PINING FOR YOU

BLUEBALL BAND OF BROTHERS #5

MARIKA RAY

PINING FOR YOU

Copyright © 2024 by Marika Ray

First Edition: May 9, 2024
Cover Model: Storm
Photographer: Katie Cadwallader Photography
Cover Artist: Jennifer Olson

Ebook ISBN: 978-1-950141-77-7
Original Paperback: 978-1-950141-78-4
Special Edition Paperback ISBN: 978-1-950141-79-1

I've been in love with my best friend since the day I met her in high school.

She was a halo of sunshine on a rainy day, pulling me out of the shadows and making me feel like life was one big roller-coaster ride of excitement. Until the day we graduated and she left on the back of a Harley with some guy who didn't deserve her, middle fingers in the air.

Twelve years later, she's back in Blueball, as if she hadn't broken my heart and never looked back. This time, she's headed straight for the courthouse to marry some goon—I mean, groom. He's clearly all wrong for her.

I decide fate has given me a second chance to tell her how much she hurt me. I bribe the guy to leave and stand in as her groom at the altar.

If I thought a marriage of convenience would be the way to pin down Rainey Shaw and teach her a lesson, I'm as dumb as the teenager who let her stomp all over his heart.

Because Rainey is back, and I'm half in love with her already.

Zeke

WHILE ALL MY friends from high school were procuring cases of beer and heading to the party at Jack's house, I was practicing my speech. I patted my pocket for the hundredth time since stripping off the suit pants from graduation and slipping into my well-worn jeans. Mumbling under my breath did nothing to calm my stomach as I paced my room. Now patting my back pocket to make sure the condoms I'd bought two towns over were ready to go tonight only jacked up my level of nervousness. I glanced at the notecard where I'd scribbled a few things to say.

Nothing made me nervous except *her*.

Rainey Shaw.

The prettiest girl at Blueball High. The life of every party. Voted best smile four years in a row by our peers. My best friend.

And tonight I planned to tell her how I really felt. All the signs were there that she felt the same way. The way she'd hold my hand with our fingers interlaced, dip her head to rest it on my shoulder, or the way her eyes would dart around a room full of people until she locked gazes with me. I also planned to give her my virginity tonight in exchange for hers.

"Zeke?" Dad stuck his head in my bedroom. "Hey, son, I don't want you drinking and driving."

I turned to face him, almost as tall as him now. He'd been my hero since the day I was born. The man was built like a linebacker and I could only hope to have his strength one day. I planned to follow in his footsteps, learning how to build all the things he did. To work with my hands and provide for my family just like he'd always done for us. He'd already been quizzing me so I'd be ready for the general contractor license exam. Now that I was eighteen, the only thing stopping me was time. With high school over, the rest of my life was about to begin. Which was why I wanted to finally tell Rainey how I felt.

"I won't, Dad. Promise. I'll stay sober and watch out for Rainey."

He dipped his head, knowing I told the truth. Everyone knew I'd take care of Rainey, even if I had to lay down my own life to do it. Sadly, it got me in trouble a lot. I'd punched at least five guys over the last four years for making lewd comments or disrespecting her.

"Okay, then, have a good time. Stay a kid just a bit longer."

He stepped forward and pulled me into his arms, whacking me on the back like he always did. I hugged him back and then we let go, walking out of my room. Dad put his arm around Mom where she waited in the living room and they both watched me go, giving me that smile they'd been giving me all day, like they were memorizing every moment of my life. I shook my head and hid my grin. They annoyed me sometimes, but I knew how lucky I was to have them.

"I'll be back late. Don't wait up."

Mom snorted as I closed the front door, Dad's bellow of a laugh reaching me out on the driveway as I approached my truck. One of them always stayed up to make sure I got home safe, no matter how many times I told them not to. I hopped in my truck and backed out of the driveway, in a hurry to get to the bridge.

Rainey and I had made the underside of the bridge at Blue-ball Park our spot. The space was mostly just a dirty cave, but the shade was cool in the summer and lent a perfect view of the rushing stream below during the winter. We'd had hours-long chats in our spot over the four years she'd lived here in Blueball. Rainey was a chatterbox, and I was all too happy to sit there and listen to her talk. The tree closest to our spot had our initials carved into it, with the number thirty right below. We'd made a pact a few months ago to get married if neither of us was married by thirty years old. Thing was, I planned to marry Rainey the second she was ready. We'd be each other's first in all things.

I got to our spot before Rainey, settling into the worn patch of dirt and weeds, spreading a flannel shirt of mine on the ground next to me so Rainey's clothes wouldn't get dirty. My fingers immediately went for my pocket, feeling the round band of gold I'd saved up for and bought a week ago. I'd seen the ring in the window of the jewelry store in town last year. It was two pieces of gold wire entwined and shaped into a ring. The second my gaze landed on it, I knew it was meant to be on Rainey's finger, symbolizing her and me, so twisted together we became one.

"Oh my God, Z! You should have seen Jedediah and Emily! They were totally sucking face right after graduation!" Rainey ducked under the bridge, words already spilling from her cherry-red lips. My hand darted away from my pocket.

"Wait. Are they dating?" I didn't care if they were dating, but I knew Rainey did.

"I guess so! Isn't that exciting!" Rainey plopped down next to me, the scent of her sweet perfume wafting over and making me melt into her side. Her curled blonde hair flicked against my arm and she placed her hand on my thigh, stretching out her legs like this cramped space wasn't big enough for her and her bubbly personality. Rainey was a hurricane, impossible to predict and deadly if you tried to contain her. "Jedediah has been drooling over her all year. It's about time he made a move."

My heart started pounding, and I knew this was my moment. I opened my mouth and made myself face my fears. "Speaking of making a move." My hand dipped into my jeans pocket, the tips of my fingers just brushing the ring when Rainey talked into the brief pause.

"I have an announcement!" She turned to me, blue eyes flashing and pink tinging her cheeks. Her excitement was contagious, even though she'd trumped my own announcement. She grabbed me by the front of my shirt and bounced in the dirt like she couldn't contain herself. My heart pounded, thinking she was pulling me closer to her. She licked her lips and I was instantly harder than a sledgehammer. My gaze darted down and then back up, wanting to be looking her in the eyes the second she told me she liked me too.

"You know that one chatroom with all the Harley guys?"

Warning bells clanged in my brain, but I didn't know how to stop her. Didn't know how to put the genie back in the bottle when he was determined to get out. This didn't sound like the announcement I was going to make, or the one I'd hoped she was about to make. Not at all.

"Hawk is picking me up tonight!" Rainey ended with a squeal and let go of my shirt to clap for herself.

A dark haze blanketed my thoughts. I could hear a bird chirping in the tree across the stream, but I was watching Rainey in slow motion, senses dulled.

"Who's Hawk?" I asked numbly, pulling my hand back out of my pocket. Without the ring.

Rainey's smile usually lit my world, but right now it was lighting a potent flame of anger in my chest that felt like it might consume me. "Hawk is the guy I told you about, remember? He's picking me up in just a few minutes!"

I frowned, lurching to my feet to get away from her perfume.

I couldn't think with it clouding my head. "You don't own a Harley."

Rainey snorted delicately and stood too, brushing off the backside of her skintight jeans. She was wearing the shirt she'd bought with her own money. The one her grandma Gertie had forbidden her to buy. Rainey's ample breasts were practically spilling out of it. The thought of some asshole named Hawk seeing her cleavage made me want to smash the bridge to pieces.

"But Hawk does, silly. And he's taking me away for the weekend to celebrate my graduation. Isn't that so sweet?"

I gaped at my best friend, fury fighting for dominance with outright concern. "How old is Hawk?"

Rainey's smile dimmed. Normally, this would get me to back off whatever I'd said to make her less than euphoric. But not this time. Not when her safety was in jeopardy.

"He said he's nineteen."

I ran a hand through my hair. What nineteen-year-old already owns a Harley? "How do you know for sure?"

Rainey shot me a disbelieving look. "He wouldn't lie about that! He's really sweet. You just don't know him."

"Exactly!" I exploded, making Rainey's mouth pop open in surprise. "No one knows him, including you, and you want to take off for the *weekend* with him? Are you insane?"

Rainey stood up straight, her breasts pressing against the edge of her shirt and threatening to flash me, and snapped her mouth shut. Fuck. She was angry. Angrier than I'd ever seen her. Normally she reserved that fiery temperament for other people. Tonight it was aimed at me.

But better that than see her get kidnapped by some asshole who lies about his age and preys on young women.

"I'm going back to Grandma's to wait for Hawk. I'll see you when I get back." Rainey twirled around and started walking away.

"Baby girl." The nickname I'd always used for her came out

like a desperate appeal. Absolute fear had trickled in, fanning the flames.

She lifted her nose in the air and kept right on walking.

"Rain!" I said, sharper this time. Still no response.

I gripped the back of my neck and looked up at the treetops, searching for an answer. I had no real control over Rainey's life. I wasn't her boyfriend or her parent. She was eighteen and in control of her own life.

Rainey had always been impulsive. Maybe even a little reckless. I'd chalked it up to her losing her dad in eighth grade. It was just some childhood rebellion she'd eventually work out of her system. But this? This was fucking insanity.

I waited until she was out of sight and then I ran to my truck, firing up the engine, and gunning it over the sidewalk to make an illegal U-turn right there in the middle of Main Street. I went the back way, pulling up to Gertie's block from the south. I cut the lights and the engine a couple houses down, sitting in my truck and watching Rainey walk into her house. I didn't have to wait long before I heard the unmistakable sound of a Harley coming down the road. Some fucker in a leather jacket put his foot down on the curb, not bothering to cut the engine or take his helmet off.

Rainey ran out the front door with her small backpack purse strapped to her. Gertie also came out the door, clearly yelling something that was probably similar to what I'd told her. The girl who had me tied in knots ignored her, climbed on the back of a stranger's motorcycle, and flipped her grandma the double middle finger while they zoomed down the road and out of sight. I sat there, stunned.

How the fuck had this happened?

Tonight was supposed to be *our* night. I was supposed to slip this promise ring on her finger and seal our love with our bodies. Tonight was supposed to be about celebrating everything that was to come now that we were adults.

I couldn't fucking breathe.

The knock on my window startled me. Gertie stood there, her eyes filled with tears. I opened the door and she immediately pulled me into a hug I couldn't return. My limbs weren't cooperating. My lungs weren't working. My brain kept flashing the sight of Rainey riding away against the back of my eyes.

"You got to let her go, son," Gertie whispered. "Let her fly and pray she comes back home."

The breath whooshed out of my lungs and my whole body shuddered. Gertie pulled back but kept her hands on my shoulders. She studied me while I fought to inhale. Fought to keep the shattered pieces of my heart inside my chest instead of spilling out onto the blacktop for everyone to see.

"Oh, honey. Rainey's like the wind. You can't catch her and tie her down. She'll only break your heart over and over again. Better to set your heart on someone else."

I finally met Gertie's gaze, seeing pain reflected back at me. I knew she meant well, but she had no idea what she was saying. My heart wasn't mine anymore and therefore wasn't mine to give away to someone else. It was already owned by the girl who'd just raced out of town without a backward glance.

I never did make it to Jack's house that night. I took the bottle of whiskey I'd planned to bring to the party after Rainey and I had time together and went back to the park. I sat on the opposite side of the bridge, staring at our spot and wallowing in pain while I sipped. I thought of all the times we sat there and shared and laughed and taken naps snuggled together. Had I really fallen in love with Rainey while she just saw me as a friend? How was that possible? How had I gotten it all so wrong?

The burn of the whiskey down my throat felt good. It gave me something else to focus on instead of the knife twisting in my chest. I hadn't quite gotten half the bottle down before the world tilted on its axis and I fell asleep right there in the dirt.

Dad found me in the early hours of the morning and dragged me home where I belonged. I spilled the whole story to him with tears tracking down my cheeks like a little boy. He didn't say much, but he took me to work with him the next day, hungover and puking my guts up. He never brought up Rainey's name that day. The physical labor soothed the rage and gave me something to focus on. Working with my hands, the burn in my muscles and the sun beating down my back, became the therapy I needed.

It was a gift that lasted a lifetime, but something I never got to thank him for.

I also never got to speak to Rainey again.

$\mathcal{R}$ainey

"MAKE sure you mop the bathrooms before you leave," my boss snapped before swirling his keys on his finger and disappearing out the back door of the kitchen.

I grimaced, knowing what was waiting for me in the bathrooms of the popular restaurant. Fresh Farm Foods was known for organic ingredients, which made it popular with all the hipsters in Denver. I just wished general cleanliness and proper aim was popular amongst the hipsters too.

"Suck it up, buttercup," I muttered to myself, wiping down the last of the counters and tossing the dirty towel into the pile that I would not be taking home to wash tonight. I'd put in my two-week notice exactly two weeks ago and tonight was my last shift. I'd stay for my allotted hours, but I'd no longer be taking work home, which was always unpaid. FFF had wrung all the labor out of me that they were going to get.

With a deep inhale for courage, I popped open the sticky door of the men's restroom and braced for nausea. Today did not disappoint. How a man with a moveable—aimable!—hose for a penis could not seem to get even one drop of pee in the actual toilet or the urinal against the wall was a life mystery I would never understand.

I squeezed my eyes shut and prayed that my weary bones would just cooperate for one more hour. One more hour and I'd be free of the last of a long string of shitty jobs. If there was a diner with a cranky boss and mold in the air-conditioning vents somewhere in the western half of the United States, odds were good I'd worked there over the last twelve years.

Blowing out a heavy sigh, I opened my eyes and attacked the bathroom with the mop until it was sparkling clean. Okay, maybe sparkling was overselling it—by a lot—but it was at least hygienic enough to pass my boss's inspection in the morning. I didn't need him taking an hour's pay off my last paycheck.

"Rainette?"

I straightened my aching back with a groan and stepped out of the bathroom. My fiancé stood just inside the door to the restaurant, his hair perfectly combed across his pin-shaped head. He had the skull shape that was made for beanies. When we'd started dating, I only saw him in warm hats, given it was winter in Denver. By the time I realized what he looked like without one, I had come to rely on him in my life. Like a comfy—yet sloppy—sweatshirt you missed when you forgot it on a cold day.

"Hey, Danny."

I leaned the mop against the wall and came over. Reaching up, I tried to give him a kiss on the cheek, but he moved backward, a grimace on his bearded face. I looked down at my hands, realizing he didn't want me to touch him. Not after cleaning a bathroom. Danny didn't like germs.

"I'm almost done and then we can go."

Danny nodded. "I've got the car all packed up." His hands dug into his pants pockets. We both ignored the sad fact that all our belongings in the world fit into one late model SUV. "You sure this'll work?"

I turned and got busy doing the last few tasks to close up the restaurant for the night. We'd gone over this a thousand times, but like always, Danny needed reassurance.

"I promise I'm not lying. I have to be married before I'm thirty and then I can inherit my dad's money." Danny grunted but didn't seem convinced. "It's all there in the prenup. Did you read it?"

Grandma Gertie had called me a couple months ago when she was cleaning out boxes in her house that was going up on the market. She'd come across the paperwork the lawyer had left with her after my father died and left me under Grandma's supervision. Believe me when I say it had come as a shock that I had to be freaking married to inherit anything. I shouldn't have been shocked. My father was an asshole his whole life, and apparently that extended even from beyond the grave.

But I was determined to be free of him, once and for all.

I just needed to get married, inherit all those zeroes, and then I'd be free to live my life however I wanted. No more shitty jobs. No more bouncing around from apartment to van down by the river. I'd made some stupid choices in my life, all in the name of exorcizing my father. He'd withheld emotion when I was a kid and I'd spent my entire twenties running after men who I thought could heal my daddy wounds. What a cliché I was. This one last hurdle would be the final thing I needed to move on as a mature adult and live my life on my own terms.

But first I needed Danny's help.

"Yeah, I read it. Signed it too."

I twirled around, hands now washed and excitement for the adventure ahead bubbling in my chest. In five quick steps I was grabbing him by the front of his organic cotton T-shirt and kissing both his cheeks. That jackpot was mine, and now that Danny had signed the prenup, no man could ever take it away from me. I'd never been happier with my stick-in-the-mud fiancé.

"Let's go get married!"

Danny shrugged, but took my hand to lead me out the door of the restaurant where I locked it and then dropped the key in the mail slot for my boss to get in the morning. A shrug wasn't exactly the reaction one wants from one's fiancé, but that was the most enthusiasm I could hope for. The man just didn't have an excited bone in his body. Which was exactly why I was marrying him. He'd require nothing from me, other than my inheritance providing a roof over our heads. Hell, I didn't think he'd even require marital relations. We'd made out a few times in the early months we'd been dating, but he never seemed that into it. Then again, I hadn't been either.

We may not be a love match in the kind of way the movies made it out to be, but we got along well enough to cohabitate. Sadly, I'd dated a lot worse than Danny. He was simply a means to an end, and while I felt a little guilty for using him in this way, I'd been completely upfront about everything. He'd agreed to this marriage willingly.

I drove the first six hours of the drive while Danny snored in the passenger seat. When I drifted into the rumble strips along the shoulder of the highway six times before jerking awake and correcting the wheel, I knew I needed sleep. Danny took over driving and I snoozed. I woke when he pulled into a small motel in Salt Lake City, Utah. We spent the night, each of us getting a twin bed. Danny didn't even blink at not sharing a bed, which was starting to make me wonder if there was something wrong with me. Or was there something wrong with him? I didn't figure it out before we both crashed in our separate beds for the night.

We woke before the sunrise and got back on the road, only stopping for snacks and pee breaks at random gas stations. When I saw the Welcome to Blueball sign in the distance, my breath caught in my throat. I hadn't been home since I was eighteen. A heavy blanket of anxiety weighed me down, stealing some of the excitement that had been with me across three states.

"What?" Danny asked, glancing over at me.

Apparently I'd made a noise in my throat. I pointed to the sign as we approached. "We all got prom pictures in front of that sign. Don't know why, but it was a thing all the teenagers did."

Danny grunted, but didn't say anything.

The first few businesses came into view, and I stared out the window at all the things that looked the same and quite a few things that looked so different it was hard to imagine this was the same town I'd spent four years of my life. And then I saw Blueball Park, the railing of the bridge over the stream barely visible through the trees. I gasped, a flood of memories coming back to me.

"Zeke and I used to spend so much time at this park," I found myself whispering.

While my teenage years had been tumultuous at best, Zeke had been my one soft spot. My person who I could trust to always be there for me. A pang of guilt hit me, like it always did when I thought of Zeke. He'd deserved a better goodbye than the one I'd given him at our spot, but I'd been head strong and, quite frankly, a brat. He'd tried to talk sense into me, but my eighteen-year-old self was not having it.

"Oh my God." I cracked up laughing, seeing Blueball Endless Eternity, the local funeral home. The undertaker there had always dressed up the place super spooky on Halloween. Zeke had had to put his arm around me in order to get me to trick-or-treat there. I explained all that to Danny, who grunted again before taking a left at the streetlight.

We had reservations at a place called Glamper's Paradise for the week. Grandma had her house on the market and had moved into a senior facility, so we had nowhere else to stay. The reviews I'd looked up online had been glowing.

"That's Ice Hill!" I nearly broke my finger on the window pointing out the steep hill off to the side of the road where we'd zoomed down on a block of ice. "Zeke was so pissed when I went down by myself before he could get on the block right behind me."

"Sounds like you were quite in love with Zeke," Danny finally said, breaking his nearly three-hour record of single-word replies.

I looked away from the memories zooming by my window to study Danny as he drove. "No way. Zeke and I were best friends. I already told you about him."

Danny shrugged and slowed down as we approached the glampground. "I guess. Just sounds like he was pretty important to you and yet you don't talk to him anymore. Seems like there was a breakup you haven't told me about."

I scoffed, feeling irritated that he was questioning me. I was also feeling irritated because I'd spent the last twelve years feeling guilt and shame over the way I'd left Zeke. I'd wondered almost every single day if he was still in Blueball. "No breakup because there was no relationship. I just moved out of town. That's all."

Danny turned into the parking lot and maneuvered the car between two trucks. It was dark out again and not enough streetlights out here in the outskirts of Blueball. "If you say so."

"I do say so," I snapped, pulling off my seat belt and getting out of the car.

I sucked in a lungful of mountain air that held a tinge of sea salt located so closely to the ocean. Being outside was life giving. I was starting to feel claustrophobic being in the confines of the car for two days straight. Probably why Danny's comments had gotten under my skin. A little time apart wouldn't hurt. The sound of music drifted over with the shift in wind. I looked around the bed of the truck parked next to us and saw lights off in the distance.

"I'm going to see what's happening over there while you check us in. I'll be right back."

I didn't bother waiting for Danny's response. He hated live music and crowds anyway. As I got closer, the music got louder. I loved this song! I made my legs move faster, careful not to step on any pinecones, but getting to the edge of what looked like a fun party in the middle of the woods. A band was up on a mini stage and plenty of people were either chatting on the picnic benches or dancing on the scarred wood dance floor.

"It's good to be back home," I muttered, feeling my old self come to life again. I stepped onto the dance floor and let my arms fly up in the air as my hips began to shake.

I was one step closer to being free. One step closer to living the life I always wanted, on my terms. And that deserved at least one dance to shake my ass and remember that even if my joints felt ancient, I was only twenty-nine. I had plenty of life left to live. I'd marry Danny, get that inheritance, and then set up a life where I didn't have to worry about every penny I spent. I wouldn't be chasing men for validation any longer. I'd finally be Rainey Shaw, without all the baggage of my father hanging over my life.

CHAPTER THREE

eke

I FUCKIN' hated these things. Loud music, obnoxious people, and light beer. Absolutely disgusting.

But I came every single Friday night. Because Paisley and Gannon asked me to. And Lord knew I didn't have enough friends to turn down a social invite.

My life was simple: I worked a physical job, I came home to my dog and a hot meal, and I went to bed. Repeat. Some might say my life was boring or unfulfilled or lonely. I'd say they added unnecessary complications as a distraction from the fact that they actually craved simplicity. Potato, po-tah-to.

I'd just turned thirty. I built my house with my own two hands and it was paid off. I helped others in my community with my skills. And I took care of my mom by making sure she got out of the house and lived a little. I had everything I needed and zero distractions.

Until tonight.

Standing as far away from the dance floor as I could get

without one of Paisley's friends dragging me out there to shuffle my feet until I could escape back to the shadows, I took another sip of this piss water they called beer. When my head came back to neutral, my gaze settled on a new figure on the dance floor. She was short, blonde, and curvy in all the right places. Her long hair swung behind her as she shook her ass in painted-on blue jeans. Her hands were in the air like she had not one care in the world.

I grunted, squinting to see her better. Interesting. Very few women in the last decade had caught my eye, and this one had definitely caught my attention. I took exactly one step closer and she spun around in time with the music. That's when my simple world fell apart.

"Rainey."

I said her name like a prayer and a curse all rolled into one tiny woman I wanted to sweep into my arms while simultaneously strangling.

I blinked and then rubbed my eyes for good measure. She was still there, oblivious to the fact that my boots had turned to cement. I was rooted to the spot, staring at her like she was some kind of apparition. Or a demon disguised as an angel sent back to Blueball to wreck my life.

The song changed and her face lit up into a brilliant smile as the new song got going with an even faster beat. It felt like time had somehow shrunk back to when I was eighteen and mooning after the one girl who was oblivious to my feelings. And that made me angry.

I'd done a lot of work on myself to get over Rainey. I'd driven hours just to go to a book store where no one would know me so I could buy self-help books and journals and shit. I'd listened to fucking meditations and guided imagery just to get her out of my head. I'd even burned her picture in some sort of symbolism that did nothing to mend my heart. Here she was, out there dancing so carefree, like she hadn't completely shattered my heart twelve years ago.

I. Was. Pissed.

Because Rainey was back, and I was half in love with her already.

Anger unfroze my feet, and I stormed across to the dance floor to loom over her. She was even prettier now, the round, youthful cheeks hollowed out to a strong cheekbone structure. Her dark lashes fanned her face with her eyes closed and there was a diamond piercing winking from the side of her nose that hadn't been there at eighteen. Her breasts had developed further and her waist had tapered. She'd gone from every teen's wet dream to every man's dream woman.

"What the hell are you doing here?"

My gruff voice startled us both. Rainey's eyes flew open and her hips ground to a halt. Her arms slowly drifted down to her sides, the soft smile on her face fading into a familiar scowl. I'd seen that final expression in my dreams for years after she'd left town, wondering if I'd done everything I could to stop her. If I should have done more. If I should have ignored Gertie's advice and gone after her.

"I'm sorry. Is Blueball no longer a free country?" she snapped, hands going to her hips. Her cheeks heated and her baby-blue eyes flashed.

Ah. Some things hadn't changed. Rainey still had a backbone and no filter on her mouth. She was fuckin' stunning, and I hated myself for even thinking it.

"It's a free town, but there's no room here for people who ditch it for twelve years without a forwarding address."

Rainey folded her arms across her chest and I gave my eyeballs exactly half a second to take in the breasts that were straining against her simple black tank top.

"I didn't realize they made you the people police since I left." Rainey lifted a single eyebrow before spinning on her sandals and marching off the dance floor.

The back of her head was a familiar sight. Still fuckin' hurt though. "Typical. Rainey walking away," I muttered, just loud enough for her to hear me.

She spun around, now walking backwards, but still away from me. With a defiant lift of her nose, she shot me two middle fingers.

Well, now that was kind of funny. The corner of my lips itched to smile, a ghost feeling from twelve years ago. "Also typical."

She rolled her eyes, but just before she turned back around, I caught the beginnings of a smile on her face too. Didn't stop her from walking away from me though. Again. I lost her in the crowd, and while more than half of me wanted to go find her, the one smart brain cell I had left that wasn't under her spell, yelled at me to stay put.

I stared at the last spot I'd seen her, already wondering if I'd imagined the whole thing. Lifting the bottle of piss water, I wondered if maybe the bartender had spiked it with something. Surely I wasn't the only one who saw Rainey just now, right? I was going to be real pissed if I'd lost my mind this young.

The crowd parted just enough for me to catch a flash of long straight blonde hair. Someone walked across and cut my line of sight for a second and then they were gone, leaving me a pocket of space to see I hadn't lost my mind just yet. Rainey had her hand on some douchebag's elbow, pulling him away from the jam session. The pale fellow looked like he worked behind a computer somewhere but played with a hacky sack in his free time in order to feel young and relevant.

Marlo, one of Paisley's friends, came barreling into my side, her hands gripping my bicep like she thought I was going to start a fight or something. There was only one person who deserved to be punched in the face and that person was me.

"Of course she has some poor guy with her. Probably gonna break his heart too," I muttered.

"Follow me," Marlo said, dragging me over to the bartender and buying two more bottles of piss water. She handed me one and I drank it down in one long gulp. Then I took the other one and drained that one too.

"Friends don't let friends drink alone."

I pulled my gaze from the crowd where I'd been staring at nothing. Vander, Marlo's boyfriend, had two more beers in his hand and a look of pity I fuckin' hated. Everyone in Blueball had given me that look for a full six months after Rainey left.

"Prepare to get wasted, then, my friend." I grabbed a beer out of his hand and gulped it down. At this rate, I'd have to pee before I got drunk enough to forget that Rainey was back in town.

Marlo held her hand out, looking at me like an irritated school teacher. Belatedly, I realized she'd asked for my keys. I thought that was a little overkill—who gets drunk on light beer? —but I gave them to her anyway. Which ended up being a good thing because not long after, Gannon, Lincoln, and Boston ditched the stage and came over too.

"Time to hit the mobile mancave," Gannon said, clapping me on the shoulder.

The five of us left the jam session in the hands of Paisley with her own playlist pumping through the speakers. As each step brought us further into the dark and quiet of the night, my shoulders relaxed. I had no idea what the mobile mancave was, but anything was better than loud music, obnoxious people, and light beer. And possibly bumping into Rainey.

Lincoln pulled keys out of his pocket when we approached a tiny trailer from the fifties that had been painted a navy blue. The Blueballer softball team logo was front and center, painted in white with two round and fuzzy light blue balls hanging from the plant.

"Still think we should petition a better logo," I said, willing to talk about any mundane topic to get my mind off Rainey. I was the official pitcher for our town softball team, but the logo had always bothered me.

"We need something badass. Like a puma. Or a cheetah!" Gannon agreed with me.

Lincoln unlocked the trailer and flipped on the lights. The inside was better than the outside of the trailer. Just long leather couches lining the sides, a flat-screen TV mounted on the wall, and an oversized refrigerator. Boston opened the appliance and my night got a whole lot better. Nothing but lagers and IPAs in that fridge. Not one fuckin' light beer in sight.

"Praise Jesus," I muttered, stepping up into the trailer and grabbing two beers, one for each fist before taking a seat. The guys all grabbed beers and someone flipped on the television to a hockey game. We drank in companionable silence, chatting here and there about nothing and everything.

I got to that point of inebriation where you soften up to the level of a heated marshmallow before I opened my mouth. "Thanks for drinkin' with me, boys."

Vander lifted his beer in the air, a little unsteady even though he was sitting down. "True friendship is when we can be opposite directions but still drink together."

Boston grunted. Lincoln started giggling like a preschooler. Gannon just looked at Vander like he'd lost his fuckin' mind.

"What the hell, man?"

Vander waved his hand through the air. "You know what I mean."

Gannon shook his head. "No, I really don't." Then he turned his perceptive gaze my way. I wasn't too drunk to realize I was about to get the shakedown. "What's the story with you and Rainey? None of us grew up here, so we don't know what's happening."

I let my head drop to the couch cushion behind me and let out a groan. There was no use fighting it. They'd either get the story from me or from someone else gossiping about me. I'd rather they get my version.

"Rainey moved here before freshman year after her dad died. She didn't tell me much about him but I got the sense he was an asshole. She was impulsive and reckless, but so damn happy. You'd smile just being next to her, you know?"

Gannon was intently studying me. Lincoln was smiling in encouragement. Boston looked like he understood but didn't want to interrupt. Vander had the flashlight on his phone on so he could make bunny shapes on the wall with his fingers.

"We became best friends, doing everything together. I fell head over ass for her and figured she felt the same way."

"Oh shit," Gannon muttered.

"Shit is right." I pointed my can of beer at him. "I was going to tell her after graduation. Had a promise ring I'd saved for and everything. But she chose that night to climb on the back of some guy's Harley and ride out of town. Never saw her again. Until tonight."

"Damn, that's cold." Lincoln whistled.

Boston just shook his head. "We should switch to whiskey."

Vander jumped up and nearly cracked his head on the curved wall of the trailer before righting himself and reaching for the short cabinet over the fridge.

"I'll stick to beer. I got a baby at home," Gannon said.

"Yeah, me too. Keva would kill me if I slept here tonight and left her with our kiddos. Saturday is her one day a week to sleep in." Lincoln shot me an apologetic look.

"Totally understand," I said, even though I had zero knowledge of what it took to raise a baby. Let alone two.

"I'll have some whiskey," Boston piped up. I fist-bumped him and then accepted the glass Vander handed me. Vander kept pouring and I kept throwing them back, each doing what had taken me twelve years of manual labor to accomplish.

I didn't remember a whole lot more from that night, but I do remember waking up the next morning with a pounding headache. My arm was numb where Vander was sleeping on it, cuddled up to it like my arm was his personal binky. Boston's T-shirt was wrapped around Vander's head like he'd auditioned for the part of Rambo at some point that night. My own shirt was balled up under Boston's head while he slept on the floor. My mouth felt like I'd spent the night sucking on a cotton ball.

Pulling my arm from under Vander, I grabbed my shirt and snuck out of the trailer, wincing at the bright morning sun. The trees swayed and I wasn't sure if that was due to a slight breeze or my own dehydration kicking in. If my heart weren't still in such turmoil over seeing Rainey, I might have appreciated the guys sticking with me last night even more. As it was, I faced the day with both dread and the world's worst hangover.

I decided to suck it up and walk home. I would feed the dog, check my mail, and get busy on a project around the house. And if Rainey and her reason for being back in Blueball kept pinging through my brain, I wouldn't let on.

ainey

THE GLAMPGROUND WAS CHARMING, peaceful even, but I wasn't getting the full experience after my run-in with Zeke last night. Instead of sleeping in and enjoying the birds chirping in the trees outside the camper door, I was stewing about last night. Can't a girl take one freaking minute out of the last twelve years of complete and utter bullshit to enjoy herself without a blast from the past ruining it with his attitude?

And his ridiculous body.

Jesus. That had come as a shock. Zeke wasn't the boy I'd known in my youth or the image I'd carried around in my head ever since. Sure, the blue eyes were still there and his thick hair that was always slightly mussed was also familiar. But everything else had changed. Zeke was all man now with those thick thighs and manly chest looking like it wanted to bust out of his T-shirt like the Hulk. Had he spent every minute of the last twelve years lifting weights?

I shook away the lusty thoughts that had no business running through my head while I lay in bed next to my fiancé. Throwing on a pair of jean shorts and a T-shirt, I quietly stepped outside and shoved my bare feet into my sandals. The place was still. Quieter than any of the places I'd lived since I left Blueball. With some cash in my back pocket, I turned toward the front of the glampground and began to walk. If my directions were sound, downtown was only a little over a mile away. Maybe some early morning exercise would push the encounter with Zeke out of my brain.

It was working too, the light sheen of sweat on my brow reminding me that summers were hot back home. I still considered Blueball home, even though I'd run away from it like I didn't care. This had been the only town where I experienced people who loved me. Grandma loved me, though we weren't what I'd consider close. My immaturity in high school had made sure of that. But everyone around town had been kind to me too. Had I been just a bit more mature, I wouldn't have left Blueball in the first place.

I tiptoed around yet another trailer, pretty sure the main driveway into this sprawling place was just past it. Although all the pine trees were starting to look the same to this city girl. My steps were light in the quiet of the early morning, which was probably why I ran into a wall of flesh just around the corner of the trailer. A bit-back curse hit my ears while I felt the ground tilt. Then strong hands were gripping my arms and pulling me upright. I stared up into the handsome face of a very pissed-off Zeke Burns.

"Wow. You look like shit," I said and then winced. My mouth would be the death of me. I'd burned a lot of bridges with the words that came out before my brain had a chance to censor them.

Zeke huffed and let me go, like my skin burned him. I wrinkled my nose. He really did look like shit if shit was the most attractive man I'd seen in more than a decade. His hair was past its usual sexy dishevelment that had driven the girls wild in high school, and he smelled like a whiskey distillery. His jeans were wrinkled and his scruffy jawline had a crease down one side like he'd just woken up. If I wasn't mistaken, he had the imprint of an ear on his bicep. Somehow he convinced me hungover looked hot. Probably because his shirt was clutched tightly in his hands and he made Chris Hemsworth look like a guy who never lifted a weight in his life. He grunted, and I took that as agreement.

"You an alcoholic now?"

Zeke did a double take, then huffed like the suggestion was unbelievable. I mean, it had been twelve years. Anything was possible. He could be a circus performer with a bad case of alcoholism or the Peeping Tom degenerate of the town. I had no idea because I'd left without a backward glance.

"You know nothing about me anymore, Rain."

His voice slipped over jagged rocks and a canyon of sorrow. Guilt, familiar and slippery, lined my skin with goose bumps in the warm early morning sunshine at the use of the nickname. No one else had ever called me Rain. Just Zeke.

I shrugged away the pesky feelings and turned toward the elusive exit of this glampground. "You're right. Forget I said anything."

Footsteps lumbered behind me and then Zeke was by my side, beefy arms pulling a T-shirt over his head. I stole a glance at a torso stacked with muscles, a light sprinkling of hair going down the center. The cotton covered it all up and I snapped my gaze back to the uneven ground ahead of me. I had no business eyeing another man's body and certainly not one belonging to my childhood best friend.

"What are you doing here?" he asked, the timbre of his voice doing things to my insides. I needed coffee and a bagel in my stomach before I could handle adult-Zeke's voice.

"What are *you* doing here?" I rebutted, ever the child when backed into an awkward corner.

Zeke shook his head, a movement I only caught out of the

corner of my eye because I couldn't get myself to look at him straight on. "I live here, dumbass."

My lips quirked, but I fought the smile. I'd almost forgotten how we used to tease each other mercilessly. It was all in jest, but I wondered if perhaps the name-calling was a little more than teasing this time around. Twelve long years can do that to a neglected friendship.

"I got that part. What are you doing *here*? As in, the glamp-ground?" We walked past the sign welcoming glampers and finally got onto the paved road that led into town.

"Marlo took my keys and I drank all the alcohol in Blueball."

I snorted and Zeke huffed what I hoped was a small laugh. "So you *do* have an alcohol problem."

"I have a Rainey problem," Zeke muttered under his breath so low I almost didn't catch it. Almost.

I cleared my throat and increased my pace. We probably had a mile to go until we hit downtown and I couldn't fathom this conversation lasting the whole way without us going down memory lane. I wasn't sure my heart could handle that right now. It was one thing to assume someone you cared about hated you. It was another thing entirely to know for certain they did.

"So, what's your answer?"

I opened my mouth to say I had no idea what he was talking about, but I knew the dumb routine wouldn't work on Zeke. So I shrugged and spilled the truth. It was scarier than any fiction I could think of anyway.

"My father left me his inheritance. Far as I knew, the only stipulation was I had to be thirty years old. Grandma Gertie called me a few months ago with some bad news. She found the paperwork as she was cleaning out her house and discovered there's one more pesky stipulation."

I could feel Zeke leaning in closer. Oddly, his presence still comforted me. Twelve years hadn't diminished that power.

"I also have to be married."

Zeke quit walking right there in the middle of the road. I turned back to see him glaring at me. I held my hands up.

"Hey! I didn't make the rules! My jackass father did."

Zeke shook his head and came back to my side. I could feel the temper rolling off his body in waves. We continued walking to town.

"Anyway, she said she was sorry she'd forgotten that part. Back then she figured I'd be married at eighteen anyway, so she forgot about it." I did not confess that the reason she thought I'd be married was because she thought Zeke would have been my husband.

Zeke stopped walking again. At this rate I wouldn't get my hit of caffeine until lunch and that just wouldn't do. I had a ton of things to get done today if I planned to be married tomorrow.

"Do you remember our pact?" Zeke asked, staring at my shoes.

I frowned. We'd made a lot of promises and pacts over the four years we'd been inseparable. "Uh..."

"The tree, Rain. Our initials. What was below our initials?" Zeke was firing words at me, clearly not needing coffee as badly as me right now.

I pulled my hair off my neck to let the breeze cool me down and thought about it. "Uh, well, the tree by our spot?"

Zeke dipped his head once.

My face brightened. I'd forgotten because it was just a silly pact kids make and then forget about. "Oh yeah. We said we'd get married at thirty if we hadn't married anyone else."

Zeke ran his hands through his hair, making it stand up in weird spots. Like a woman had just run her nails along his scalp. Tight muscles strained against his T-shirt while his eyes burrowed into my skin. The sun was rising behind him and for a hot second there I thought maybe I was seeing some kind of angel, if angels inspired lust and looked like they wanted to pull on your hair until you groaned.

"Your birthday is in five days," Zeke said from between clenched teeth.

"Don't remind me," I said, rolling my eyes. This was why I needed the caffeine ASAP. I had a quickie wedding to plan and it had to go off without a hitch.

"Let's get married."

"I have to get a license, flowers, and a dress." I started listing off all the things I needed to do before Danny and I could get down to the courthouse to do the deed.

Then his words sunk into my brain.

"Wait, what?"

Zeke looked positively feral. "Let's get married, Rain."

My mouth dropped open and I couldn't have closed it even if a fly had flown right on in. I reached up and rubbed my eyes. Zeke was still standing there, looking like he was about to fight some unseen enemy, but his gaze was trained on me.

"Did you just ask me to marry you?" I was shocked, definitely. But I was also just a teensy bit gleeful. Zeke, the quiet hot guy from high school who all the girls secretly wanted, wanted *me*?

"No, Rain. I didn't ask you. I told you to marry me."

My whole body let out a little shiver at his tone. Fuck me, that was hot. Teenage Zeke had never used that tone of voice. Ever. Believe me, I would have remembered.

"Okay."

Zeke lost just a fraction of the angry glare. And that's when I remembered my sleeping fiancé back at Glamper's Paradise. What was his name? Oh yeah. Right. Danny.

"Wait. Shit. No, I can't."

Zeke stormed right up to me, that feral look back with a vengeance. "Why not?" he growled.

I looked up—way up—into his eyes and told him the truth. Even if saying it out loud made me cringe inside at how wrong it felt.

"Because I'm already engaged."

CHAPTER FIVE

eke

I WASN'T KNOWN to be a hot-tempered guy. The customer was always right, grannies should be helped across the street, and a long run with Daisy, my golden retriever, was enough to work out any frustrations before they came out in the form of a fistfight.

Except when it came to Rainey.

"You're engaged?" I spat the words, not even wanting them in my mouth, let alone swirling in my brain.

Rainey. Engaged. To someone else.

I'd envisioned her married before. Assumed she would be after twelve years apart, but seeing it with my own two eyes was straight torture. That douchebag last night must be her fiancé.

Rainey dropped her arms and smiled, but it was more of a wince. "Yes. Danny. I'm marrying Danny. Hopefully tomorrow if I can get all the details worked out today." She hitched a thumb over her shoulder. "Which is why I need caffeine. Bucket size if they have it."

"Don't do it." The words slipped out before I had a chance for my pride to rein them back in.

Rainey sighed. "I have to, Zeke. I need that money."

"There are other ways."

She shook her head and her gorgeous hair flicked around her shoulders and arms. "I have no time. It has to be tomorrow."

"I'll stop it." I would. I'd move that fuckin' mountain over there to stop her from making this mistake. "Do you even love that guy?"

Rainey's eyes flashed. Good. Maybe she'd feel even a fraction of the anger I felt right now. "You don't understand. Danny is harmless. He signed my prenup. It has to be him. I won't find anyone else in the next five days."

"I'll sign your prenup. Marry me instead."

Rainey's mouth dropped open, her cheeks starting to blush. Then she was rolling her shoulders back like she was seven feet tall instead of barely five feet. "You're crazy."

She whirled around, all that thick blonde hair twirling in the breeze behind her as she marched off. I opened my mouth to say something—anything—that would make her change her mind. But then I remembered the stubborn streak that ran right through her logical brain, obliterating common sense. Rainey didn't listen to reason, that much hadn't changed.

But I had.

I'd let her go once and look what that got me: a shattered heart and twelve years of wondering if she was still alive.

I wasn't going to let Rainey go so easily this time.

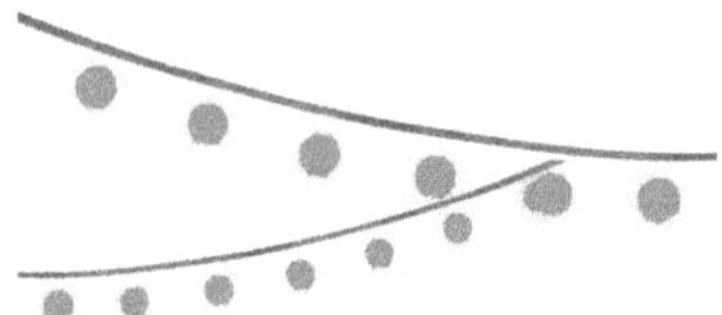

"You're my girl, aren't you, Daisy?" I buried my face in her neck, scratching behind her ears like she loved so much. This girl had been with me for six years now and I couldn't imagine not waking up to her horrible dog breath every morning. One wag of that tail and I found myself rolling out of bed far earlier than I planned based on how long I'd been up the night before. At least I wasn't hungover this time.

Daisy's tongue swiped across my cheek, as if to agree with me. I let her go and stood up, pulling on a pair of pajama pants and walking her outside the back door. She ran out ahead of me and did her business on the wide expanse of green lawn while I hit the button to start the coffee pot. After I'd calmed down yesterday and gone for a run with Daisy, I'd ditched the hangover and come up with a plan. I had important shit to do today and not much time to do it in.

One thing stood out during our conversation yesterday. Rainey hadn't said she loved her fiancé. The only reasons she'd listed for marrying him was the prenup and that inheritance. Had she claimed to be madly in love with him, today would look a lot different. I would walk away and let her marry the douchebag.

But she'd claimed no such thing.

I clapped my hands and Daisy came running back inside. I got her fed and cracked some eggs into the frying pan for myself.

While those cooked, I poured my coffee and gulped it down so fast it burned my mouth. Daisy sat in the middle of the kitchen staring up at me while I bit back a curse.

"I know, I know. I'm just in a hurry," I told her, carrying on in conversation like we did every morning. I swore she understood me.

I plated the eggs and didn't bother to sit while I shoved them in my mouth. Of course, I dropped some and Daisy pounced before the clump of egg even hit the hardwood. Thanks to her my floors were sparkling clean. The plate clanked as I nearly threw it in the sink in my hurry and grabbed an apple, biting into it as I ran back to my bedroom. Daisy followed, barking as if we were playing a game.

My closet held exactly one suit and normally I loathed it. It was the suit I wore when all of my friends got married. Considering the whole town knew each other and invited everyone to their wedding, I'd had to wear it a lot the last few years. But today, I was wearing it for me.

I grabbed my keys and crouched down at the door to the garage. "Daisy, girl. You be good while I go get your mama." Daisy cocked her head to the side. "I know it's just been you and me, but we're making room for one more today, okay?"

Daisy licked my face and I took that as a yes. I held out my hand and Daisy bopped her paw against it, a little trick I'd taught her years ago. Another kiss on the top of the head and I was out the door and sliding into my work truck. A few stops later in town, I had what I needed.

The brick facade of Blueball's courthouse was a focal point of the town. The building was old, but it had been kept up nicely. The bronze plaque out front told the history of our town, complete with a picture of the old man who'd planted all the bluebell flowers for his late wife, mistakenly calling them blueballs. The name had stuck and the hideous logo was born.

I checked my watch, surprised to note my palms were sweating. This had to work. If my plan failed, I'd lose Rainey forever.

Again. The way I saw it, I lost her twelve years ago, but fate put her back in my path for a reason. I couldn't fail this time.

A late model SUV pulled up to the courthouse and a man in an ill-fitting suit climbed out of the driver's seat. The guy tugged on his sleeves and then fumbled with his short tie. Couldn't be more douchebag if the word was stamped right on his tall forehead. Okay, the guy wasn't that bad, I just didn't care for his significance to Rainey. She was far too good for him.

And now it was showtime.

"Hey there," I called out real friendly-like. I forced a smile on my face and lifted a hand in greeting. "Are you Danny?"

The guy looked at me with suspicion, but then stretched his arm out anyway. We shook hands and I wanted to laugh over the limp grip. This guy was all wrong for Rainey. She'd steamroll right over him.

"Yeah, that's right. I'm Danny. And you are...?"

"I'm an old friend of the family. Rainey's, that is." I put my arm on his back and steered him closer to the large tree that cast a decent shadow on the west side of the courthouse in summertime. Just in case Rainey showed up early, I didn't want her to see me talking to her fuckin' fiancé.

Danny swiped at his damp forehead, drawing attention to his nervousness. I took heart in the fact that I was about to help this poor guy out of a situation he wasn't sure he wanted to be in. Pulling my hand back, I reached into the inner pocket of my suit jacket and pulled out one of those little envelopes the bank gives you when you withdraw a significant amount of cash. Danny's eyes widened on the thick white envelope.

"I've got a deal for you, Danny, one I know you won't be able to resist." I clapped him again on the shoulder and the guy winced before shrugging off my hand.

"I, uh, actually don't like a lot of touching," he mumbled. "Too many germs."

"Sorry." I could respect that. But I also wondered how that was working out for Rainey. I could clearly remember an endless string of evenings when she'd snuggle with me in the dirt at our place under the bridge. Germs were the last thing on her mind.

"I'll keep this short." I waved the envelope between us. "I have ten thousand in cash right here. It's all yours if you just get back in that car and leave Blueball."

Danny's wide-eyed gaze bounced between the envelope and my face, trying to gauge my sincerity. I flipped my thumb through the edge of the bills so he could see it was all there. My savings account had taken a serious hit, but it would be worth it if this worked.

"Ten thousand? To leave Rainette? Like, forever?"

For a quick second I worried the poor guy really did love Rainey. Why else would he balk at the cash? When he tugged at the hideous red-and-gold tie around his neck, I figured I'd better give him more reason to leave.

"Don't worry, Rainey will still inherit her money from her father. I'll make sure of that. Believe me, this is more than you'll get if you marry her. You signed the prenup, right?"

Danny nodded, still staring at the cash. "Uh-huh."

"So, do we have a deal, Danny?" I didn't want to rush the guy but I wanted to be done here before Rainey showed up.

His head lifted and I could practically see the dollar signs in his eyes. "Do you need me to sign something?"

I shook my head. "I trust you, Danny. Just take the money and head on out. Leave Rainey behind."

"Done." The guy plucked the envelope out of my hand and hurried back to the curb where he left the car waiting. With one foot inside, he swiveled back. "Can you, uh, tell her I'm sorry?"

"Absolutely," I assured him. lying through my teeth. I lifted my hand goodbye and he was off. I would do no such thing. Mostly because Rainey was going to be so pissed off I wouldn't be able to get a word in during her tirade. I watched until his brake lights turned a corner and were out of sight. "Phase one done."

I didn't have to wait long before another car pulled up to the curb in front of the courthouse. This one was a rideshare blasting country music. I bent down to see the driver. Yep, it was Jaxson. That kid made more money than most college graduates just driving people to and from the airport.

The back door opened and Rainey climbed out. Time slowed down as Rainey swirled to wave goodbye to Jaxson. Her blonde hair was curled, hanging down her back except for two little braids on each side that tied at the back of her head with a pale pink flower. Her white sundress flared out as she spun, showing off her gorgeous legs ending in a pair of wedge sandals that made my mouth water. She looked amazing. More beautiful than prom our senior year when I'd almost had heart failure at her blood-red dress with the high slit up one leg.

Jaxson peeled away from the curb and I felt the exact moment Rainey's gaze fell on me. I could always feel her presence, like the cells in my body functioned differently when she was in my atmosphere. Her broad smile slowly fell as she looked around the empty sidewalk.

"Zeke?" she asked, walking closer. "What are you doing here? Where's Danny?"

Up close I could see how she'd taken time with her makeup this morning. Unlike yesterday morning when she hadn't had a lick of makeup on, her skin had a range of colors on it now. Black eyelashes and some sort of color on the lids made her eyes look even more doe-like. Her bare shoulders were kissed with just a hint of pink, as if she'd been out in the sun longer than she should have been yesterday.

I dreaded the next few minutes, knowing I'd be crushing her plans, but I knew it was for the best. She'd still inherit her money and she'd eventually get over being mad at me. Fairly certain she'd get over it.

"He's gone."

Rainey simply blinked up at me, her thick lashes fluttering. "Excuse me?"

"Danny," I said helpfully. "He's gone."

Her hands came to her hips. "What do you mean, he's gone?"

Time to come clean and face the firing squad. "I know you said he was perfect for you, but the man didn't even pretend to protest when I offered him money to leave Blueball."

Rainey's mouth opened but no words came out. Her eyes had gone stormy and that red splotch on her neck didn't bode well for my longevity.

"You. Did. What?" she snapped.

I leaned in, wanting her to understand what a terrible choice he was. "I offered him money, Rain. And he took it. What kind of douchebag—"

Her hand came out of nowhere and struck my cheek. My fuckin' molars shook with the force of the slap. Shit. I shook my head a bit to see if that would clear the fire ants marching across half my face. Rainey didn't wait for me to explain further, she just turned on her heels and made a run for it. She was surprisingly fast for the tall footwear she sported.

"Rainey!" I called after her.

This time, she didn't look back or even bother to flip me off. The bride was just gone.

CHAPTER SIX

Rainey

THERE WERE people in your life who you were supposed to be able to trust. A father was one of them. Sadly, that trust had been squashed long ago when it became clear my father cared more about his career than he did his only daughter. Little girls don't realize that sometimes unwanted pregnancies happen, and as much as I loved my father back then, the love was not returned. All I knew was that Dad was constantly annoyed with me and even that attention was only when he deigned to acknowledge my existence.

Which led me to Zeke. He'd been a respite for me when my father passed away and I'd been moved to an unfamiliar town to live with my grandma. I'd trusted him as much as a girl who'd learned not to trust anyone could. I knew I'd hurt him when I up and left Blueball without a backward glance, but to ruin my future so thoroughly just because I didn't mail home a postcard every now and then? To butt his nose into my life when I was finally one tiny step away from not having any man determining my fate like I was some puppet on a string?

To say I was livid would be a gross understatement.

Heads swiveled as I ran through downtown on the sidewalk. Moms with their little ones running errands turned to stare. Shopkeepers lifted an arm in a hello I could not make myself return. My eyes had glazed over with a sheen of volcano red so vibrant I could barely make out where I was running. And these damn shoes! While they were the most attractive footwear I had —a splurge over a year ago when I'd gotten a rare Christmas bonus—they were not built for a sprint. I took one wrong turn at the new pergola built in the middle of the park, but with a quick dart around a park bench, I was able to get back on track.

I slid to a halt in the wet mid-morning grass, my lungs burning almost as much as my eyes. The bridge lay before me, a recent coat of stain making it shine as beautifully as the day I'd left town. The trickle of the stream below hit my ears as it always did in this spot, but everything else was unfamiliar.

Instead of a patch of flattened grass leading to dirt underneath the bridge, there was an ornate wooden bench, clearly a hand-carved work of art. The patchy grass had been replaced with a small field of wildflowers that would have taken my breath away if I hadn't already been doubled over trying to breathe. It was gorgeous. And also not the spot it used to be.

"I thought I'd find you here," came a deep voice from behind me.

My spine snapped straight. I squeezed my eyes shut and tried to figure out the conflicting emotions swirling in my chest. I was so mad at Zeke right now. I was sad our spot had been changed over the years, becoming something else entirely. It was like our entire friendship had been erased, and while I'd done a fine job of that by disappearing, seeing Zeke again had made me wish for a friendship like that. Combine all of that with a touch of panic about how to still inherit that money and I welcomed the new bench as I sank down onto it.

Zeke moved closer, but he didn't sit next to me. "About a year after you left, I built the bench. The city let me install it and plant the wildflowers."

"Why?" I asked, numbly. From my perch on the bench, I could just barely see the stream and the matching wildflowers on the other side of the embankment. It was a beautiful view and far more comfortable than when we'd wedged ourselves on the rocky ground as teens.

"In the off chance you ever came back home," Zeke said simply, like that explained everything.

My head dropped and the first tear rolled down my cheek. He was so sweet, and yet I desperately needed that money. He didn't understand what he'd done.

"I'm so mad at you." It was barely a whisper, not one lick of fight behind the tone. So unlike me I scared myself. If I didn't have that fire burning bright in my chest, I wouldn't have survived the last twelve years. It couldn't fail me now.

Zeke didn't answer right away. He slowly moved around the bench and had a seat next to me, taking over most of the space on the wood slats and forcing me to hug the side. The man had certainly grown since he was eighteen. I was mad at him, but I desperately wanted to rest my head against his shoulder and just breathe him in like I used to. He used to make me feel so safe.

"And I'm mad at you, Rain," he finally said.

I nodded, still not able to look at him. I was afraid if I looked up into those eyes, I'd either say something that would further damage any friendship we'd had or I'd beg him to rescue me. Neither of those options would improve my situation. A bird tweeted from the tree above, perhaps irritated we'd interrupted her morning.

"What are we going to do?" I asked, genuinely curious if our friendship could be revived. Or if I wanted it to at this point. He'd just screwed me out of close to a million dollars.

Zeke turned toward me, the bench creaking below us. His

knee bumped mine, causing my gaze to fly to his face. The wedding crasher was smiling.

"We're going to go back to the courthouse and get married. Duh."

I stared at him like he'd grown another head. Teenage Zeke had been cute with his shy smile and steady confidence, but grown-up Zeke was absolutely gorgeous. In that suit, he should be gracing every magazine cover out there. His hands were big and scarred and told a woman he knew how to work with his hands. His hair reminded me of a hockey player, a little too long to be considered stylish, but somehow dangerously attractive. I was embarrassed to admit that it took me this long to understand why he'd shown up at the courthouse in a suit. The man planned this whole thing.

"Why are you doing this?"

Zeke didn't answer. He stood and offered me his hand. Without thinking, I slid my palm against his, shocked at how right it felt to let him pull me to my feet just like old times. He didn't let go right away either, instead inclining his head toward the nearby tree. I knew what tree he meant. I'd spent an hour one afternoon carving our initials into it when we were seventeen. It did not escape my notice that I'd also carved the number thirty below our initials.

Fuck. That stupid pact.

"You're serious?"

As was his way, Zeke didn't answer with words. He tugged me up the embankment and back onto the soft grass of the park before letting go of my hand. He was careful to slow his long gait as I navigated the expanse of lawn in wedges that weren't made for a stroll in the park. He'd always been considerate like that, a trait I had taken for granted until I went out there in the real world and saw what sorry excuse for men were single.

We finally made it to the sidewalk and Zeke put his hand on my back to steer me in the direction of the courthouse. This time, as people raised their hands or voices in a hello as we walked by, Zeke waved back and I tried to smile. Considering they'd all seen me sprint through here just moments earlier, I felt a little foolish now. Some of the faces looked familiar, but now was not the time for reminiscing and catching up.

Zeke stopped us next to a faded blue truck parked outside the courthouse that had seen better days. He opened the driver's side door and leaned in while I waited on the sidewalk. I glanced up and down the street, my brain spinning a million miles a minute. Was I really going to do this? Marry my old best friend just to inherit some money? I could feel the seconds ticking away like sand through an hourglass while I debated what to do. My birthday was in four days. There was no way I'd find anyone else who would marry me. Not without me having to pay them off, which would defeat the whole point of inheriting a stack of money. I needed that cash to start a new life.

"A bride should have flowers on her wedding day. Something your douchebag fiancé should have thought about."

Zeke stepped back on the curb holding a simple bouquet of wildflowers tied with a white ribbon, much like the flowers down by our spot. He handed them to me while I clutched them to my chest and wondered why my ribs ached from this simple gesture. When was the last time a man had given me flowers? I wracked my brain and came up empty.

His hand warmed my lower back again as he ushered us up the steps of the courthouse. His other hand grabbed the handle of the glass door and I dug my heels in, my hand gripping his bicep as I tugged him to a stop. He looked back at me, a questioning look on his handsome face.

"Why are you doing this?" I repeated. I needed to know, needed to understand what was in it for him. Did he want my money? Was I so pathetic that he was willing to put up with a short, fake marriage to help me out of a tough spot? My pride had taken a beating over the last decade, but I still had some left.

Zeke looked away, scanning the street. "I watched you, Rain.

All four years I knew you, I watched you. I observed how you lit up when people paid you attention. I saw how much you needed that attention and I figured it was because your father never gave it to you. You wouldn't tell me about it, and that was my fault for not being someone you could fully trust. Probably because I was just a dumb kid with stars in my eyes and a lack of impulse control when it came to you."

When he mentioned my father, I felt like I'd been stripped naked right there on Main Street for all to see my childhood wounds. I sucked in a deep breath. Zeke didn't talk much, but when he did, I always listened because it was usually something important. Maybe that's why Zeke was so insightful. He didn't chatter constantly like other people. He saved all that energy for observing people. He saw more of me than I cared for.

Zeke's gaze swung back and nearly glued me to the ground with his intensity. His voice came out low, intimate in the way it scraped across the air between us. "But you're back now. And I'm no fucking kid."

My knees began to shake. He dipped his head until he was looking at me from my height. I couldn't have looked away even if I wanted to. "I'm marrying you because you deserve to know what it's like to be someone's everything. Even just once in your life. And I can give that to you, baby girl."

Then he swung open the door and pushed me inside the courthouse.

eke

I KNEW what it felt like to have a broken heart. Mine was crushed twice, one right after the other when I was still a teenager. I also knew it was possible to keep right on living with your heart severed into pieces. Somehow, you just limped along with the pieces working enough to survive, but never sewing back together again.

This? Marrying Rainey so she could inherit her dad's money?

This was going to break my heart all over again.

Knowing it didn't change my decision, however. As I mulled it over last night, I realized my love for her wasn't something I could choose. I couldn't shut it off after it had begun. Believe me, I'd tried. Neither time nor distance had made that love falter, and now that she was back, she needed me. Of course I was going to be there for her. Even if it broke my heart all over again. Might as well go out in a hot bonfire of brokenhearted-ness and live out the rest of my life in the ashes.

As we stepped into the waiting room for the judge, I got

Rainey seated on one of the chairs while I went to the side table where they displayed refreshments. I couldn't stomach any of the donuts offered, but I needed one of their square white napkins. Grabbing the pen used for checking in, I scribbled out a simple sentence and signed my name. Coming back to the chairs, I handed the napkin to Rainey.

She glanced up, looking stricken but so damn pretty she made my lungs constrict. Her lashes lowered and she studied the napkin. I thrust it at her and she took it, her head bowed over it as she settled it in her lap next to her bouquet of flowers.

Whatever possessions Rainey brings to this marriage before, during, or after are hers to keep.
Zeke Burns

"It's not a fancy prenup, but hopefully it calms your fears." I had a seat next to her, wishing I could take her hand in mine. If I had my way, this marriage would be very different. One hundred percent real and there would be no moment in time where I wasn't touching her.

"Thank you," she whispered, folding the napkin and tucking it into the top of her dress.

The door next to the check-in desk opened and a woman my mother went to bible study with—Whitney? Willa?—poked her head in, reading from a clipboard. "Rainette Shaw and Danny Day?"

My head jerked toward Rainey. "You agreed to become Rainey Day?"

She looked up at me finally, her lips rolled inward as she stifled a laugh. I shook my head.

"Damn. I really did save you."

Rainey lost the fight and let a wide smile take over her face. It almost felt like we were eighteen again, sharing some inside joke while the world went on around us.

I held my hand up in the air, but didn't take my eyes off Rainey. "There's been a change in grooms."

"Zeke?" the woman asked, clearly confused.

I stood up and offered my hand to Rainey, looking over my shoulder. "Yes, ma'am. I'll be the groom today." Was her name Winnie? Wanda?

Her eyes were comically huge behind her wire-rimmed glasses, her mouth dropped open in surprise. Ah ha! Wendy was her name. Wide-eyed Wendy. Her gaze darted to our joined hands and she snapped her mouth shut.

"Well, I'll be," she muttered. Then she smiled brilliantly at us both. "I always thought you two would get hitched one day!"

Rainey let out a giggle that was tipping toward hysteria. Not wanting this to get any more awkward than it already was, I pulled Rainey through the door with me, giving the woman a polite smile.

"Thanks, Wendy."

She ushered us into the judge's office, blathering on about how cute we were in high school while Rainey blushed and kept making that weird giggling noise that sounded like she was choking. I just wanted to hurry up and get this ceremony over. If it had been our real wedding, I'd have wanted it to last forever. Under the circumstances, all I cared about now was making Rainey mine. Even if she thought the whole thing was temporary.

Before I could strangle Wendy and her chatter mouth, we were standing in front of the judge, holding hands and repeating his short vows. Wendy kept Rainey's bouquet safe as she hovered behind us. Rainey's hands were shaking as I held them. I gave her a squeeze for encouragement.

"Did we bring rings with us today?" the judge asked me.

Rainey inhaled sharply at the oversight, but I'd spent four years of my life covering the pesky details that went along with her impulsive decisions. I let go of her hands and reached inside my suit jacket to the inner pocket that held the rings.

"This is my father's ring. I hope it's okay if I use it." I held up the plain gold band between us.

"But…" Rainey searched my face for an answer to her unspoken question about why it wasn't on my father's finger.

When my head dipped like it always did when I thought of my father, Rainey sucked in a shaky breath and wrapped her hand around mine. When I looked up, there were tears in her eyes. She nodded once, grief and understanding shining back at me. I gave the ring to her and she held it reverently in her hand for a moment before slipping it onto my ring finger as she repeated the vow the judge supplied.

My heart, the one that barely limped along these days, suffered another blow seeing that ring on my finger. While he wouldn't approve of a temporary marriage, my father would understand my enduring love for Rainey. That was how he'd always felt about my mother. I reached back into my pocket and fished out the last two rings. I held out the diamond ring I'd bought this morning, slipping it onto Rainey's finger as she gasped again.

"Engagement ring," I said, then slid the twisted band of gold I'd kept for twelve years in the back of my dresser drawer onto her finger also. "Wedding band." I repeated the vow and then held her fingers tightly as she stared down at our hands.

When she lifted her head, right as the judge pronounced us husband and wife, there were twin tracks of tears sliding down her cheeks to pool against her lips where she held a soft smile instead of a look of fear.

"You may kiss the bride, son." The judge, a man I'd known my whole life, shot me a wink and clapped me on the shoulder.

My heart galloped in my chest, putting on quite the effort for being broken. Perhaps the pieces didn't understand that this situation had an expiration date. This marriage wouldn't last, so there was nothing to get excited about.

I'd dreamed about kissing Rainey so many times to the point I wondered if the real thing could ever live up to my expectations. As I took one careful step closer to her, the judge and wide-eyed Wendy as our witnesses, clutching her hands to her chest a few feet away, it all faded away. I let go of Rainey's hands and cupped one hand beneath her jaw. She tipped her head back, her eyes nearly as wide as Wendy's.

My thumb swept across her smooth cheek and collected her tears, as if I needed to feel the liquid against my skin to make myself believe this moment was actually happening. Her tongue darted out to wet her bottom lip. Pink stained her cheeks. I dipped my head and breathed her in, that sweet fruity scent of hers swirling through my brain and bending time. I could have been eighteen again, begging her silently for a kiss that would never come. Rainey's eyelids went heavy and slid shut.

With barely an inch between us, I closed the gap, my lips finally touching hers for the first time. I froze, all finesse and talent out the window, but then Rainey responded, her lips softening under mine. A groan threatened to spill from my throat and I tilted her head to deepen the kiss. My other hand gripped her waist. My tongue teased her bottom lip, and for a second, her body tensed against me. Then she melted, her breasts pressing against my chest as her body conformed to mine. Her lips parted and I took advantage, my tongue sweeping in to taste her. I wanted to know every part of this woman and it started with consuming her mouth. My arm slid around her waist and not one inch of space could be found between us. My brain went to a place where all I knew was Rainey. Her heady scent, her little moan in the back of her throat, her tongue tentatively touching mine.

A deep chuckle brought my awareness back and I ended the kiss with a soft pluck at her lips. Regret already filled my veins, not of the kiss, but of having to end it. I'd probably never get the chance to do it again. I knew without a doubt that kiss had ruined me for any woman in my future. Rainey's eyes were still closed as I pulled back. She was breathing hard. Her entire body leaned against me, as if her legs had decided to quit working.

The judge clapped me on the shoulder again. Rainey's eyes blinked open, unfocused. "I marry a lot of couples and the kiss tells me everything I need to know. You two are going to make it."

And with that proclamation, he turned to walk away. Wendy was ushering us out of the office in a rush, handing the bouquet back to Rainey and offering us her congratulations.

We stood alone on the steps of the courthouse, blinking into the midday sunlight, our hands still clutched together. We both turned and looked at each other at the same time. I imagined my face held the same shock and confusion as Rainey's. She licked her lips and my brain went fuzzy, hoping she still tasted me there.

"Um..." she whispered, cheeks flaring beyond pink and into red hues now. "What now?"

A deep sense of satisfaction settled in my chest, like a key that I'd held forever had finally found the lock it was made for.

"We go home, wife."

CHAPTER EIGHT

*R*ainey

YOU DESERVE *to know what it's like to be someone's everything.*

That line, said in Zeke's deep grumble of a voice, lived rent-free in my brain, repeating over and over. Surely it was mocking me. I was the last person who deserved what he offered so freely.

I felt like my head was stuck in a frozen cloud hovering somewhere above my body. My limbs were moving like a normal person, but my brain wasn't computing anything that had happened since I pulled up to the courthouse and Danny was nowhere to be found. Thankfully, Zeke seemed fully operational, taking charge of the situation and tugging me along with him.

A deranged giggle escaped my mouth when we pulled up to the trailer Danny and I had been renting. Zeke looked over from the driver's side of his truck.

"You okay?"

He'd asked me that already. Twice. I couldn't blame him though. Our normal roles had been reversed. I'd gone quiet on the ride over here and he kept up the one-sided conversation with inane facts about the town of Blueball. Usually I was the one with crazy schemes and hijinks that got me in trouble, along with a motormouth that hated a beat of silence. Today, Zeke had jumped into the fray like he might have learned a trick or two from watching me back in high school. The switcheroo in personalities was mind bending.

I shook my head and studied him, all handsome and calm behind the wheel. "You just fucking *married* me."

He shot me a lopsided grin and held up his left hand, showing off his wedding ring. "Yep. Sure did. Now let's get your stuff and move you over to my place."

My brows furrowed. "Wait, what? Why?"

His eyebrows matched mine. "We're married. You can't live by yourself in a trailer. That might be suspicious."

That made a lot of sense. I just hadn't thought this through yet. My brain was still stuck on the plan I'd had with Danny, which was now in shambles. We'd planned to stay in the trailer for a week, make sure I got my money, and then we'd head out on our next adventure. I'd promised him a roof over his head for the next five years in exchange for marrying me. We'd already lived together for two and I had zero plans of actually settling down with a whirlwind romance, so I couldn't see the harm in helping a friend out.

"Yeah, okay," I muttered, climbing out of the truck before Zeke could come around and help me down. He followed behind as I climbed the two steps into the trailer. The place felt even smaller with his shoulders filling the doorway and blocking the sun.

My head was on a swivel and I was shocked to see that all of Danny's things were gone. On the counter, right by the sink that still held my dirty plate of toast that I'd eaten early this morning to calm my stomach was a note in his barely legible handwriting.

Sorry.

Zeke muttered an expletive under his breath. I blinked, feeling ashamed that Zeke saw the note. What kind of loser of a woman has a fiancé that will take a bribe and ditch her the morning of their wedding? The answer was clear and instant: the kind that doesn't deserve to be someone's everything.

"I'll grab my things," I said quickly, moving into the back of the trailer just to get away from Zeke for a moment. I needed to breathe and think through everything without being in his airspace. Zeke made me want to lean on him like a damsel in distress and let him take care of everything. If the entirety of my life had taught me anything, relying on other people was a sure-fire way to lose everything that mattered. The only person I could rely on was me.

It didn't take me long to throw my clothes and toiletries into a suitcase. The rest of my things that had been in the back of Danny's SUV were stacked on top of the kitchenette table. At least Danny had the decency to leave my things before he ditched me. When I came out of the bedroom, Zeke had already moved all of my things to the back of his truck.

"Ready, wife?" He had to duck to fit in the trailer, but he was smiling like this trailer, this day, this wife of his, wasn't the most inconvenient thing that had happened to him. He took two steps to reach me and pulled the suitcase from my hands. With his other hand on my back, he urged me toward the door. "How do you feel about dogs?"

"Huh?" Again. Brain not working. Conversation skills were gone.

"I have the goodest good girl at home. She's going to lick you 'til you push her off of you." Zeke threw my suitcase in the back of the truck while I tried not to shiver at him talking about a good girl and licking me. Don't even get me started on his calling me "wife."

Perhaps my body somehow got some wires crossed and thought this marriage was real. I'd be smart to remember that it wasn't. Zeke opened my door and stepped back so I could climb in. Even that little gesture made my stomach swoop around like a schoolgirl with her first crush. Danny had never held a door for me. I definitely didn't need him to, so why did Zeke doing it make my heart thump?

The drive over to Zeke's house was marginally better. I managed to string together answers that were more than a single word. The neighborhoods had changed, obviously, since I'd lived in Blueball, so most of our conversation was about that. He made a left onto a long gravel driveway that led to a white shiplap house with shutters framing the windows. The wraparound porch was the stuff of architectural dreams. I couldn't help comparing it to the tiny one-bedroom apartment I'd shared with Danny.

"Welcome home," Zeke said, sliding out of the truck and coming around to help me out while I gaped at his property.

"This is yours?" I glanced around at the land surrounding the place. I had zero frame of reference for measuring land, but it looked like he had at least an acre to go with the house.

"Sure is. Built the house myself. With the help of some friends for some parts, but it was mostly me." Zeke hauled my suitcase out of the back of the truck and then his hand was on my back, ushering me up the five stairs to his porch. I felt like he'd been doing that all day, just pushing me around to where I needed to be. It should have annoyed me. I certainly wouldn't have let Danny, or any other man for that matter, push me around, but with Zeke, it felt less like telling me what to do and more like taking care of me when I was unable to do it myself.

Zeke opened the front door—a gorgeous light wood double door—and a reddish-blonde mass of fur bounded out. She skidded to a stop and sat on her haunches, tail sweeping the entire front porch while she whined from the back of her throat.

My face split into a smile, and when I let her sniff my hand and she licked it immediately, I buried my face in her neck and gave her a hug. To my surprise, she lifted up her front paws and laid them on my shoulders as if she understood the need for a hug.

"Oh, aren't you a sweetheart?" I murmured, scratching her back and behind her ears.

Zeke's chuckle broke us apart. "Told you Daisy would like you instantly."

I kept petting her, even as I stood back up. "Thankfully I'm only allergic to cats. Dogs are way better anyway."

Zeke shrugged and whistled for Daisy to go back inside. "I think so, but that's only because cats don't generally take to a leash and go on runs with humans."

So that was how he stayed in such phenomenal shape. I followed Daisy, stepping inside Zeke's house and immediately coming to a stop. The place was gorgeous. Warm tones, lived-in areas, and just enough light coming in through the tall windows to make you feel like nature surrounded you. Zeke stepped around me and wheeled my suitcase through the living room and into a hallway. I hustled to keep up, thinking he'd show me to my room and I could get changed. Instead, he wheeled my suitcase right into a large bedroom that had a rumpled bed. The covers had been tossed over the bed, but not tucked nicely. Basically, the bare minimum needed to say you'd made your bed. Pretty much what I'd done every day I'd lived with Grandma Gertie.

"I made some room in the top drawers over there and the closet is only half full anyway, so make yourself at home," Zeke said, letting go of my suitcase and taking off his suit jacket. Daisy ran over to a doggie bed by the window and curled up, though her eyes tracked my every move.

Alarm bells rang out over my sudden awkwardness. "Oh, I can't possibly take your room." I would only be here a few days anyway. No need to kick the guy out of his own bedroom.

He was already shaking his head. "I only have the one bed and you're not sleeping on the fuckin' couch. I'll sleep out there if you want."

Dumbfounded, I looked back down the hallway to the living room. The couch wasn't more than an oversized love seat. "You won't fit on the couch."

Zeke shrugged and began to unbutton his dress shirt, a line of tan skin being revealed with each button. My gaze followed the movement until I realized I was ogling my best friend. "It's fine. I can sleep anywhere. Floor will work."

I shook my head. Zeke had been so kind. Well, other than scaring off my fiancé. But he'd given me a diamond ring, saved me from losing my inheritance, and now was giving me a place to stay for a few days. Surely I could compromise a bit.

"It's okay. We can share a bed." I laughed, but it felt strained, even to my own ears. "Not like we haven't done it before."

There'd been plenty of nights in high school when he'd snuck into my room and spent the night when I asked him to. Nothing had ever happened, of course, though if Grandma ever found out, she would have grounded me.

Zeke pulled his shirt off and tossed it on the bed. My eyes had no choice but to drop down his body and take in the chest and abs and arms and shoulders that had most definitely not looked like that when we were eighteen. I'd already seen him shirtless just yesterday, but the change was still startling. Holy cow, Zeke had grown into the kind of man you saw on the movie theater screen. I swallowed hard.

"Uh, yeah, okay. I'm just going to go change." And like a total coward, I grabbed my suitcase and hightailed it to the first door I saw. Sadly, it was the closet, not the bathroom, but I went inside anyway, slamming the door shut behind me just to get away from the half-naked sight of Zeke. The door closing put me in total darkness however, and I had to fumble around until I found the light switch.

I opened my mouth and screamed silently into the closet. The secret outburst helped ebb the nerves that were frayed from today's events. I was so embarrassed, I wanted to find a shovel and dig my way out of this town, never to be seen again. Why was I awkward like this? It was just Zeke out there. My old best friend. No need to drool all over him.

It was the lack of sex. That had to be it. Danny didn't have a strong sex drive. Hell, we hadn't even slept together. He claimed we were waiting to be married, but I think he just wasn't much interested, which was fine by me. I wasn't much interested either, but that meant it had been years since I'd had sex. That was it. I was just sex deprived. That's why even my best friend looked like a tasty snack. Surely I could hold my shit together for a few more days. Then I'd leave Blueball and find my own life. And a boyfriend with an actual sex drive. Or a really nice vibrator.

"I'm going to make us a late lunch. Meet me in the kitchen when you're done?" Zeke called from the bedroom.

I stood up straight and smoothed my hair over my shoulder. "Sure!" I called back, voice wobbling.

"Fucking pull it together, Shaw," I told myself under by breath before opening my suitcase and changing into my oldest sweatpants and the baggiest T-shirt I owned. I absolutely would not think about how his closet smelled like him: generic soap and a faint whiff of cologne. Leaving my stuff in a neat pile in his closet, I meandered out to the kitchen where Daisy skid across the tile floor to get to me.

Zeke was in a pair of shorts and a T-shirt, his feet bare. "There's a container of treats over there if you'd like to give her one." He pointed his knife to the opposite side of the kitchen. I got one out and had her sit, then gave it to her. I could have sworn Daisy smiled at me before she bent her head to crunch on the treat.

"So, you have a dog and a house. What else is there to know about grown-up Zeke Burns?" I asked, leaning back against the countertop and trying to ignore how good he looked even in casual clothing.

"What do you want to know?"

Everything. "Well, for starters, what do you do for a living?"

"I'm a contractor. I mostly work on people's homes in Blueball and surrounding area, everything from small jobs to building a custom house." He spun around with a stacked sandwich on a plate. "You still hate mustard?"

I took the plate, touched he remembered my aversion to the yellow goop. "Thanks. I do. Evil stuff."

Zeke picked up his own plate and waved at me. "Let's eat out on the porch."

We sat on the white wood furniture out front, the chairs rocking back and forth as we ate. His neighbors were fairly far away, most of the lots in this area looking like estates with plenty of land in between. The sandwich was the best thing I'd eaten in weeks and the conversation flowed easily. Maybe this wouldn't be so bad. I could use the next few days to catch up with Zeke and patch up our friendship, and then I'd be gone before I lusted after him so much it made things awkward.

Over an hour had passed before the first lull in conversation. Zeke looked at me and pressed his lips together.

"What?"

He ran his teeth over his lip and the gesture brought back a flood of memories. He'd done that before every big test. Or when he had to be social and he didn't want to. Zeke was nervous.

"So, when's our expiration date, wife?"

eke

I WANTED to stay lost in the delusion of Rainey being my wife. I mean, she was, but in my head, sitting there chatting like long-lost friends, my brain started to latch on to the fantasy that my future had panned out the way I'd always wanted it to. Me and Rainey. Together.

But eventually, reality butted its way into my brain and I had to face facts. Nothing about this marriage was real. Not in any way that actually mattered. Rainey's fingers twisted in her lap as she contemplated my question.

"I'm not sure," she said quietly. Her voice lacked the usual bubble of excitement. I wasn't sure I ever heard her talk without some sort of passionate emotion behind her voice when we were teens.

I frowned, wanting to slap myself on the forehead for thinking Rainey would be exactly the same as when we were kids. Of course things had changed. I'd certainly changed, right? I didn't examine that question too deeply, afraid I'd find the same quiet kid with a soft spot for one particular girl. Rainey swiped at her forehead and I instantly stood. It was insanely hot in the summer here in Blueball. Especially in sweatpants.

"How about we head inside and give you time to unpack and relax? Been a crazy day."

Rainey gave me a soft smile and stood, heading inside with her empty plate and mine. Daisy dragged herself from the shady patch at the back of the porch and stretched, following us inside with a grateful head butt to the back of my hand. Rainey put the dishes in the sink and then spun around there in the kitchen, the two of us looking at each other awkwardly.

"I've got a, uh, project, out back." I pointed aimlessly somewhere toward the back of my property. "How about I get to that while giving you time to rest?"

The relief on Rainey's face made me feel both miserable and good. Good that I'd saved her from the awkwardness that suddenly fell between us all alone in my house, and miserable that time away from me made her relieved. That's how things had always been between us. I bent over backwards for her and she went along her merry way, never knowing that I loved her more than life itself.

"Okay, sounds good. I'll probably unpack and then catch a quick nap. I didn't sleep well. Nerves and all that." She made a noise like she was trying to laugh but it fell flat. Then she spun on her bare foot and practically ran out of the room.

I squeezed my eyes shut and wondered what the hell I'd gotten myself into. For now though, Rainey was happy, in my house, and not married to the douchebag. That would have to be good enough for me.

Summer had no mercy and I was drenched in sweat when I noticed the sun was dipping in the sky. I'd spent several hours clearing a space out back for a future pergola, a project I hadn't had any intention of getting to this year. I lifted the bottom of my T-shirt and wiped my face. My hands ached and my muscles were fatigued. Maybe I'd be able to find sleep tonight after all. I looked up at the sky and said a quick thanks to wherever my father was, something I found myself doing often. He'd taught me how to use my body to burn off negative emotions, a skill that had come in handy yet again. Dropping my tools in the shed I kept along the fence line of my property, I came in through the back of the house and stepped out of my dirt-covered boots.

The house lay silent, not even the claw scratches of Daisy running to greet me. I used the kitchen sink to wash my hands and arms before venturing to my bedroom. The door was ajar, so I nudged it open. Rainey yelped at the squeak of the door and twirled around in head-to-toe flannel. The material had ice cream cones of various colors all over it.

"You do know it's summer, right?" I drawled, using humor to try to cover the insane desire that swept through me from seeing her in innocent pajamas. The things were practically birth control with how hideous and juvenile they were.

Daisy's tail thumped from over in her doggy bed. I gave her a look that told her I wasn't happy with how quickly she'd ditched me for Rainey's side. She let out a whine and got up, coming over to sit on my feet.

Rainey shrugged, her cheeks pink with either embarrassment or heat exhaustion. "Yeah, but it's all I brought with me. Denver is definitely cooler than Blueball."

I crossed my arms over my chest. Something wasn't adding up. "You brought flannel pajamas for your honeymoon?"

Rainey's gaze dropped from mine. "Hey, I made soup. You didn't have much in the fridge, so I made what I could for dinner. Hope you don't mind. I put your bowl in the microwave. I wasn't sure when you were coming back."

"Answer the question, Rain."

Her head snapped up and her eyes went wide. "You know, you didn't use to use that tone of voice with me."

I huffed. Thank God something about me had changed over the years.

Rainey sat on the edge of the bed. The same side I slept on, but I didn't make mention of that.

"Danny and I weren't like that."

I narrowed my eyes, something in my chest lighting up like someone had struck a match. "Explain."

Rainey threw her hands out, clearly exasperated. "We never slept together! We were friends. Kind of. I mean, we were engaged, but it was mostly just for my inheritance. At least on my end."

Daisy pushed her weight against me and I almost fell over. After taking a step back and righting myself, I stared at Rainey like she'd grown an extra head. "Didn't you live together?"

"Yeah," she said quietly, still not looking at me. "For two years."

I couldn't help the laugh that filled the silence between us. The twin spots of color in her cheeks deepened. "I knew he was a douchebag, but that's next level."

Rainey pulled her legs up under her, looking small and defeated. "I started to wonder if something was wrong with me."

The laughter faded in an instant. I was also across the room and standing in front of her before I registered that I'd moved. "There's not one thing wrong with you, Rain. That guy was a—"

"Douchebag. Yeah, so you've said."

I cupped my hand under her chin and pulled her head up until she looked me in the eyes. "There's not a single thing wrong with you, Rainey. You two just weren't right for each other, that's all."

She lifted an eyebrow. "So you're telling me that you'd live with a woman for two years, share her bed, and even if you weren't right for each other, you still wouldn't sleep with her?"

"I'd never invite a woman to live with me if we weren't right for each other."

The understanding that she was now living with me, however temporary, hit her after a few seconds. She swallowed hard, and I let go of her face to step back.

"I've had a few girlfriends over the years, but nothing serious. I can tell you from a guy's perspective, the problem was him, not you."

Rainey scooted back on the bed and leaned against the headboard. "No serious girlfriends? Come on, Zeke. You were lusted after by pretty much every girl in high school."

I squatted down to ruffle Daisy's fur, wishing I'd never seen Rainey in my bed. I'd never get the image out of my brain. "No, I wasn't."

Rainey sat forward, energy crackling from her once again. "Yes, you were! I know of, like, twenty girls who liked you at one time or another!"

I waved that ridiculous idea away and asked what I wanted to know. "How about you, wife. Any serious boyfriends I need to know about?"

Rainey stilled instantly, sitting back down, face wiped of all emotion. "Nope. Nothing serious."

There was more to the story, that much was obvious, but Rainey didn't look like she was ready for story time. Suspecting something happened to make her choose a nonthreatening guy like Danny made every protective instinct I possessed take up arms. Instead of trying to drag the story out of her and therefore becoming yet another man she couldn't trust, I stood and walked to the doorway. "I'm going to heat up the soup and then take a shower."

"Okay." Rainey picked up a book from the bedside table that hadn't been there before. She opened it and began to read, ignoring me entirely. I walked out, wondering when Rainey had picked up reading. In high school, I thought she might have been allergic to the ink with the way she avoided them at all costs.

Rainey was still reading when I hit the bathroom to shower. When I came out again in a pair of shorts and not much else, the light was off. She had rolled to her side, barely hanging on to the edge of the mattress while she slept. Or pretended to sleep. I wasn't quite sure. It was for the best anyway. It would be easier for me to sleep if I knew she wasn't also lying there in the dark, aware of my presence and too afraid to say anything. Rainey had never been skittish before, a change that made my hands clench into fists. Someone had hurt her. Maybe even more than her father.

Before this marriage fizzled, I was going to find out who it was and hunt them down. She may not be mine in the way I wanted, but she was still my wife.

I lay there for hours, just listening to her breathe and watching her sleep. Almost couldn't believe she was right there next to me. My arms ached to hold her, but I couldn't reach for her. I wouldn't. Not when this marriage was a sham. It would already hurt bad enough when she left. Adding in the comfort of her touch would certainly kill me.

Sunrise came and somehow I'd found sleep in the early hours of the morning. I stiffened, seeing an empty spot where Rainey had been sleeping. My heart thundered, my brain instantly going to the only scenario in life that scared me: Rainey had left me already.

Then her bubbly laughter filtered into the bedroom and my lungs whooshed out a breath of relief. Not gone. I heard my mother's voice and I squeezed my eyes shut with a groan. Not gone. Just in the kitchen talking to my mother.

Fuck.

Fuckin' small towns and their gossip. I should have expected this, but as per usual, Rainey had struck me dumb with her presence. Mom should have been my first call after we left the courthouse. She was pretty reasonable in general, but she was going to be pissed that I'd gone off and gotten married without her there. After Dad died, she'd told me more than once that I was all she had left. And now I'd gone off and gotten married and hadn't fuckin' told her.

I rolled out of bed, ready to face the firing squad and my dog that had already gone rogue and chosen to stay at Rainey's side.

The scene in the kitchen hit me full force. The two women who mattered most in my world had mugs of steaming coffee in their hands, smiling at each other as they chatted across the small island, Rainey standing and my mother sitting on one of the two barstools. Daisy lay in another of her doggie beds in the kitchen, a bone held between her front paws while she gnawed on it. Rainey saw me first, her gaze dropping down my bare torso before snapping back to my face with guilt shining in her big blue eyes. Mom swiveled and held out her arm.

"You're lucky I talked to Rainey first. Otherwise I'd be slapping you instead of hugging you." I gave her a hug, watching Rainey over Mom's head.

"Wouldn't be the first woman to slap me. And I would have deserved it too."

Rainey winced and then took a sip of coffee. "I found some eggs. How about I make us some breakfast?"

"You don't need to do that," I muttered, letting go of Mom.

Rainey smiled, but it looked forced. "No, no. You two chat and I'll make some omelettes."

I could feel Mom watching us, her eager eyes darting between us like we were still kids and she was waiting for us to open our Christmas presents. Honestly, I hadn't seen her this happy in longer than I cared to admit. Guilt for lying to her mixed with relief that shadows didn't hover beneath her eyes this morning. I stepped around her and pulled Rainey into a hug. I felt her sharp inhale. Leaning down by her ear, I whispered to her, trying to make it look like I was simply kissing her neck.

"Play along."

Her arms came around me, her fingernails dragging along the bare skin of my back and making my eyes roll back in my head. I used another second to get my shit together before I let her go. Getting an erection in front of my mother and my fake wife wasn't on my list of things to do today.

"I'm just so happy the rumors were true for once!" Mom had

her hands clasped below her chin, smiling at us like we'd made all her dreams come true.

"You're not even mad we got married at the courthouse?" I leaned on the counter, arms braced on the cool granite.

Mom smacked my arm, but it was playful. "Oh, I'm mad about that, but I'm more happy to see you two finally together again. I couldn't ask for a better daughter-in-law."

The pan slipped out of Rainey's hands and hit the stovetop with a clatter. She offered a quick apology before ducking behind the refrigerator door to grab the eggs. I looked back at Mom, wishing for her sake too that all of this was real. Her eyes went glassy and I knew that look. She was about thirty seconds away from hugging me to her chest and sobbing. She'd done a lot of crying since Dad died, and I couldn't bear to see her crying over me.

"I'm so proud of you, son," she whispered, clearly trying to keep her shit together and failing.

The guilt hit harder then. I realized I was going to break her heart too when Rainey and I eventually split up, a consequence I hadn't thought through in my panic to make Rainey mine.

I opened my mouth to say something, anything, to make this better, but I heard the front door bang open and then voices speaking over each other. Someone—or multiple someones—had entered my house uninvited. I pushed off the counter, ready for trouble. Rainey gasped behind me and dropped an egg on the floor, making a mess. I snapped my fingers at Daisy, who'd jumped up to lick up the mess, and she sat back down on her doggie bed with a whine.

"Would you look at that? Pigs have flown and Rainey's back in Blueball!" Gertie announced, sliding into the kitchen with Milly Booth at her side. The two old ladies smirked, acting like they owned the place. And perhaps they did, because before long there were five of us having breakfast in my house.

"I'm going to go get a shirt," I managed to say.

Milly waggled her thick eyebrows behind her glasses. "Don't bother on my account, young man."

Rainey giggled hysterically and suddenly I felt naked. This morning was not going the way I had planned.

Not at all.

CHAPTER TEN

GRANDMA GERTIE LOOKED JUST the same as she did when I lived with her. We video called each other every year at Christmas, so I'd seen the way she'd changed over the years, but seeing her up close highlighted the lines in her face and the way her athletic body had tipped over the edge into thin.

I stepped over the mess of raw egg on the floor and threw my arms around her shoulders, careful not to hurt her. She squeezed me back fiercely, calming my nerves about her aging.

"Hey, free bird," she whispered in my ear, sending me back over fifteen years ago when she'd nicknamed me. The name had stuck because it described me perfectly. Moving around all these years had helped me feel like life was in my control. I wasn't stuck with an unloving parent, or sent to live with my grandma. I lived where I wanted to, when I wanted to.

My eyes flooded with tears, an unexpected reaction. I never planned to come back to Blueball, but I was already finding the visit cathartic. I gave Grandma another squeeze and then pulled back. Her own eyes were glassy as we smiled at each other like no time had passed.

"You are a sight for sore eyes. I never knew what that phrase meant until just now."

"Grandma," I muttered, not wanting to sob right there in the kitchen with an audience. My emotions were all over the place. The last twenty-four hours had been a whirlwind, and being in the presence of a half-naked Zeke was not helping me get my head screwed on straight. Thank goodness he'd vacated the kitchen to get dressed.

"Don't hog her all to yourself, Gertie," Milly said, gently nudging Grandma aside and giving me a hug. The woman barely came to my chest, which was saying something because I was short too. She'd shrunk over the years, but clearly her friendship with my grandma hadn't.

"Nice to see you again, Miss Milly."

"Oh, we're all adults now. You can drop the miss." She pulled back and shot me a wide grin. "Speaking of adults...I hear you and Zeke tied the knot!"

A warm glow spread through my system at her words. I held out my hand, showing off my two rings. All three ladies clustered around me, along with Daisy, wanting to get an up-close look while they talked over each other. I knew I shouldn't be amping up their excitement when I knew the marriage wouldn't last, but it felt good to have these women surrounding me with what felt like a lot of love.

Zeke came back in the kitchen and our gazes locked. A slow smile spread across his handsome face as he took in the scene. It was only when his mother shouted a comment about the twisted wedding band that he looked away.

"This looks familiar!"

I turned my attention to Emily. "What do you mean it looks familiar?"

She popped her head up, darting a glance from me to her son and then back to me. "Well..."

Zeke interrupted, pushing his way into the tight circle to put his arm around my waist. The ladies backed off a bit—but not Daisy who sat on my feet—realizing a little breathing room was needed. I tried not to focus on how nice it felt to be in the circle of Zeke's arm. It highlighted how little touching Danny and I had done.

"I bought that band when we were seniors. Always meant to give it to you but never got around to it." Zeke let me go. "Now who wants an omelette?"

Milly and Grandma clamored about always being up for a second breakfast, but Emily continued to frown at the back of Zeke's head. I wasn't sure what that was all about, but I wasn't going to step in the middle of a family issue when I wasn't really family. In a week or so the rings would be back in Zeke's possession anyway. Instead, I got bread and butter out of the refrigerator and helped prepare breakfast. It was as we were sitting around the table that Grandma started asking the hard questions.

"I didn't realize that you and Zeke still communicated. When I told you about your inheritance, I didn't realize that this was going on between you two." She pointed her fork between Zeke and me.

"Inheritance?" Emily asked, clearly confused.

"Yeah, Rainey is getting an inheritance from her father, but we just saw each other again when Rainey came back to town and everything clicked into place. Sure, it's impulsive, but..." Zeke trailed off with a shrug.

Emily reached over to pat his hand. "But you've always loved Rainey."

"Exactly," Zeke agreed, not looking my way.

"So, when are you going on your honeymoon?" Grandma asked.

Zeke looked at me then, a bit lost on how to answer that.

I turned to look at the ladies with a soft smile. "This was all very sudden, so we don't have anything planned. We just want some alone time to get to know each other again."

Milly snorted. "Is that what the kids are calling it these days?"

My cheeks heated while all three ladies giggled at her implication.

"Speaking of wanting alone time, I should head out. I just had to see for myself. I'm very happy for you both." Emily scraped her chair back and stood, locking gazes with me. "You always made my son smile, Rainey."

Guilt and something unfamiliar clogged my throat. Zeke reached over to sling his arm around me, saving me from responding with words. Grandma and Milly followed suit, the three of them taking their plates to the sink and then giving us hugs. Zeke helped me out of my chair and kept my hand enveloped in his as we walked them to the front door.

"I wouldn't mind a great-grandkid one of these days," Grandma said with a wink.

I laughed, but it came out like I was being strangled. Milly clapped her arthritic hands together, changing the subject.

"Oh! How about we throw you two a party? You didn't get a formal reception."

"That's a great idea!" Emily brightened and neither of us had the heart to put a stop to their plans. I didn't know if I'd be gone already by the time they put a party together. This was exactly why marrying Zeke instead of Danny hadn't been a good idea. But what was done was done. We'd just have to face the consequences now.

"We'll discuss it and let you know," Zeke said diplomatically.

There was another round of hugs and then they all left. Blessed silence overwhelmed me as the door shut and it was just the two of us once again. Zeke looked at me sheepishly, reaching up to rub his neck like he'd developed a headache.

"That was...interesting."

I bit back a smile. There was nothing funny about deceiving

both of our families, but seeing Zeke off-balance was a teeny-tiny bit funny. He projected such confidence all the time, it was nice to see he had some self-doubts on occasion like a normal person. Lord knew I had a whole suitcase full of self-doubts.

"The Auntie Brigade strikes again," I muttered.

The one side of his mouth tipped up and he dropped his hand. "Want to get dressed and I'll show you my next project out back?"

I had nothing better to do until I turned thirty in two days, and spending time with Zeke sounded like just the distraction I needed. "Sure. Mind if I take a shower first?"

"Rain. You don't have to ask permission. My house is your house now. Do whatever you'd like. Use whatever you'd like."

I shifted on my bare feet, feeling like I was going to break out into a sweat at any moment. Maybe the flannel pajamas weren't the best idea in the middle of summer. "Thank you. I guess it just feels weird to invade your space when it's…well. Short term."

Zeke inhaled sharply and changed the subject. "Go get ready. I'll clean up the kitchen."

I nodded, feeling guilty about our families, but also guilty for using Zeke's generosity for my own gain. Then again, I hadn't planned on doing that. Zeke had forced my hand when he got rid of Danny. With that last thought I rolled my shoulders back and vowed to take an extra-long shower just because it served him right to get a hefty water bill.

When I came back out of the bathroom an hour later, my wet hair was piled on top of my head and I felt like a new woman. It also helped my flagging ego to see how Zeke's gaze immediately dropped to my bare legs. The cutoff jean shorts fit like a glove, but my skin was paler than I'd like. Working two jobs hadn't left much time for sunbathing in Colorado. Zeke held out his hand and I took it, refusing to analyze if holding hands with my temporary husband was a good idea.

Daisy trotted beside us as we went out the back door and

headed for the backyard. There were trees that lined the property line, some of them bearing fruit. The grass was wild and high in most places, which meant I had to follow Zeke's exact footprints to not get lost in the weeds.

"I didn't want a manicured backyard. In the spring, the grasses bloom these incredible flowers. Seems a shame to mow it." Zeke finally stopped in the back corner where the grass had been chopped back to reveal bare dirt. "And this is where I plan to build a pergola. Once the trees grow a bit more, it'll be the perfect shady spot to relax with a beer."

"Or a book," I offered, already picturing the beautiful space once the pergola was built.

Zeke turned, a wry smile on his face. "Yeah, what's up with that? You read now?"

I scoffed, pretending I was offended. "I'll have you know I've always been able to read." I paused. "I just never wanted to in high school. Then as an adult I found they were the perfect way to escape. I could travel anywhere I wanted to in a book."

I could feel him studying me, but I refused to explain further. Our temporary marriage didn't leave time for every detail of where I'd been over the last twelve years. Besides, there were more important things I wanted to know.

Looking around the property and seeing the back of the house, I couldn't help but compare his life with my abysmal one. "You've done really well for yourself, Zeke. I'm impressed."

"Thanks," he said dismissively.

I lifted my gaze, finding him staring at me intently. Like there was something he wanted to say but wouldn't. I knew the feeling. "Tell me about your dad?"

I could see the way the topic affected him. His shoulders drooped and his eyes took on a mourning that made my stomach ache. They'd been close in high school. Zeke had looked up to his dad, calling him his best friend. Besides me, he would always add, like he wanted to assure me of my place in his life.

Instead of answering, Zeke stripped his T-shirt over his head and my mouth popped open. My blood heated and it had nothing to do with the sun beating down from the summer sky. He draped the material over the dirt patch and offered me a seat. I dropped my butt down on the T-shirt, just so I'd quit ogling him. He didn't help matters by sitting next to me, his bulk pressing into my side. We didn't really fit on the T-shirt, but I wasn't going to complain. His touch soothed me in a way I hadn't felt since I'd left Blueball in my rearview mirror. God, I'd missed this man.

"You sure you want the whole story?" he finally said.

I bumped his shoulder. "Only if you want to tell it."

I would absolutely not demand he spill his guts if he didn't want to. I certainly wouldn't be sharing everything either. We both had our secrets to keep and even a marriage license wasn't going to loosen our tongues.

CHAPTER ELEVEN

eke

PRETENDING to be happily married in front of my mother was the hardest thing I've done since I spoke at my father's funeral. It would crush her to know it was all for show, a fact I should have thought about before I paid Danny off and ran him out of town so I could take his place at the altar. But as per usual with Rainey, I'd lost my head. All I could think about was making her mine. Even if it was just for a short time.

Thing was, there wasn't a lot of pretending going on on my end. I loved Rainey. Always had, always would. I just couldn't tell her that, not when she obviously didn't feel the same way, so I hid behind the fact that I'd loved her as a friend once upon a time and that was all there was to it. I'd simply show her how I felt about her in all the little and big things I could do for her while she was with me. It would have to be enough, because in two days, she turned thirty years old.

And she would have no reason to stay with me longer than that.

Loving her felt as natural as drawing breath. I was all in when it came to Rainey. Had been at eighteen and still was at thirty. So it felt right to give her my heart for the next two days and deal with the fallout later.

"About six months after you left, Dad was diagnosed with cancer. Like a lot of men, he ignored the aches and pains, thinking he was just getting old and work was getting hard on his body. By the time he went in, it was already stage four."

Rainey cursed under her breath and laid her head on my shoulder. It reminded me so much of old times I had to stare at Daisy running back and forth through the tall grass to ground myself in the present. I cleared my throat and continued, telling the simple end to a great man.

"He passed a little over six months after that. And I was almost glad. He hated to be a frail man and that's what cancer did to him. Once he knew he couldn't beat it, he wanted to go fast." My voice quit working and that deep sorrow I could always tap into when I thought of those last days with my dad threatened to overwhelm me.

With only a sob as warning, Rainey almost knocked me over, throwing herself into my chest and wrapping her arms around my neck and squeezing tight. She lay halfway across my body, so I steadied myself and held her, appreciating someone to hang on to. Mom and I had each other when it happened, but she'd quickly withdrawn into herself after the funeral and nothing I did got her to come back out. I'd felt so alone for a long time after Dad was gone. Friends from school would offer condolences, but no one just held me. With Rainey's arms around my neck, I felt like she was holding the pieces of my shattered heart together.

Temporary, I reminded myself, *just temporary*.

We stayed locked together for so long Daisy got bored chasing squirrels and came over. She must have thought we were playing a game because she burrowed her big body between us, lashing us with that rough tongue as she broke us apart. Rainey's cheeks held tear tracks as she pulled back, a sight that made my heart squeeze painfully tight. Must have affected Daisy too because she licked her face clean, even as Rainey tried to push her off, her tears turning to laughter. I whistled and Daisy jumped off Rainey to sit by my side, looking over at me with innocent eyes. I shook my head at her antics, but she made me smile.

Rainey laid her hand on my thigh, stealing my attention from Daisy. Her big blue eyes were bloodshot and yet still so pretty I wanted to take her picture just so I could pull it out later and stare at her. "I'm sorry, Zeke. I'm sorry you lost your dad and I'm sorry I wasn't here to be with you."

I put my hand on hers and squeezed. "Thanks, but no eighteen-year-old is equipped to deal with that kind of grief. I was almost happy to go through it alone without dragging you down with me."

Rainey flipped her hand over and laced her fingers with mine, a soft smile playing on her lips. "Still wish I'd have been there." She squeezed my fingers. "Now tell me why you didn't give me this pretty ring back in high school. You were holding out on me, mister!"

I knew what she was doing. She was trying to change the subject to bring some happiness back in my life. She was constantly doing that when we were kids, saying I took everything too seriously. And maybe that was true.

My thumb swept over her diamond ring and then the twisted band. I couldn't tell you how many times over the years I'd taken it out and just stared at it, wondering about what could have been. It was almost surreal seeing it on her finger now.

"I bought it senior year. Took all my money from that extra job Dad gave me on the ol' Skinner House."

"I remember! You worked every weekend for two months and I was so annoyed with you for not being available." Rainey made a face like she was embarrassed. "If I'd only known..."

Then she wrinkled her nose, which only made her cuter. "But why didn't you give it to me?"

I ran my teeth over my lip, knowing the truth would hurt her, but deciding this was not the time for lies. She might leave at the end of the week and at least I would know I'd told her everything.

Well…almost everything.

"I planned to give it to you after graduation." I let the words hang there while she filled in the blanks. I saw a myriad of emotions cross her face, ending with her burying her head in her hands and moaning.

"But I left on the back of a Harley!" she said through her hands.

Anger simmered, a relief from the grief. "Yeah, with Eagle or some stupid fuckin' name like that."

"Hawk." Rainey's shoulders shook and I thought she was laughing. Which kind of pissed me off. Nothing about that night was laughable. Then I saw a tear slip through her fingers and I realized she was crying again.

"Shit," I mumbled, hauling her off the ground and into my lap, tucking her leg over my side so she straddled me and I could pull her in, chest to chest.

Her crying was soft, but I could feel her body shaking with it. I held her close and tried to will the tears away with my presence. I was all too aware of her bare legs hugging my hips and her breasts crushed to my chest. There was only a flimsy tank top and denim between us. Squeezing my eyes shut, I tried to focus my brain on what truly mattered: making Rainey feel better. This was not the time to get an erection, which she would most certainly feel sitting on my lap like this.

Rainey hiccuped and pulled back just enough to look up into my face. Her nose was starting to run but she didn't bother to wipe at it. Instead, she cupped my face with her soft hands and tried to smile.

"That was really sweet, Zeke. I wish I'd stuck around. My life would have been totally different if I had."

Her mouth hovered just an inch away from mine, a fact that sent flames slicking across my skin. But she didn't move closer and neither did I.

"Why didn't you stay?"

The question was out before I could pull it back. Before I could tuck it away with all the rest of the hurt that she'd caused me that we didn't talk about. I didn't actually want her to say out loud that I wasn't enough. That my friendship, my love for her, wasn't enough to keep her in Blueball.

Rainey dropped her hands to my shoulders and there was already more space between us. My heart sank, even before she opened her mouth.

"My nickname is free bird."

As if that explained everything. I knew Gertie called her that, but I never picked up that nickname because I never wanted to entertain the thought of her leaving.

Rainey stood, pushing off my shoulders and dashing her hands across her cheeks before wiping them on her shorts. Then she held her hand out to me, but I didn't take it. Instead, I stood on my own two legs, snatched my shirt off the ground, and pulled it over my head. Daisy ran circles around us, and without discussing it, the three of us headed back to the house.

We danced around each other the rest of the day, both of us finding things to do that didn't involve the other person. I got groceries while Rainey called the lawyer handling her inheritance. I couldn't be there while she discussed her timeline for leaving me. When I returned home, she was off the phone and reading on the back porch. I poured her a glass of white wine, hoping she still liked it like she had when she and her girlfriends pilfered a stolen bottle junior year. She gave me a soft smile in thanks and immediately sipped as she went back to her book. I got busy making a salad and cooking chicken on the outdoor grill. I didn't know how to make anything fancier, which I told her as we sat down to eat. Rainey said it looked like a feast and tasted even better. I knew she was lying, but I didn't call her on it.

She insisted on doing dishes, which I let her while I took a shower. It was tempting to take matters into my own hands while the hot water steamed up the bathroom. Anything to slake the sexual need that reared its ugly head anytime Rainey was in the room. Sleeping all night next to her was an exquisite torture that even whacking off in the shower wouldn't help.

The towel was tight around my waist when I opened the door. A billow of steam escaped, obscuring my view. Still, I halted immediately, stunned stupid to find Rainey with her flannel sleep shirt on. It was what was not on the bottom half of her that had me still as a statue. Hard as one too. She had nothing on except a pair of thong underwear, the perfect juicy globes of her ass aimed in my direction as she bent over the bed.

"What are you doing?"

Rainey jolted and straightened up, whipping around with a pair of scissors and her pajama pants in her hands. "Making shorts." Her voice was an octave higher than normal.

My lips quivered. The one leg of her pajamas looked like it had been hacked off by a chainsaw. "Told you it was too hot for those."

Rainey's whole face was bright red. "Turn around!"

I turned as a gentleman should, chuckling at her embarrassment, but refusing to wipe that image of her bare ass out of my brain. I'd have to live off that visual for decades to come.

"Okay."

I turned around and Rainey was already in bed, the covers up to her nose. I took pity on her and changed in the bathroom, noting that her gaze followed me all around the room until I shut the door. By the time I brushed my teeth and climbed in bed, her eyes were closed. By her breathing, I could tell she was asleep. Leaning over carefully, I placed a whisper of a kiss against her forehead. Then I lay there next to her for what felt like hours before I fell asleep.

At some point in the night, she cuddled up against my back, her toes finding warmth against the back of my calves. Again, I lay there for over an hour, just feeling her against me and wishing I could turn over and pull her close.

Maybe, just maybe, we could stay friends when she left. I wasn't sure how my heart could handle that, but my heart was hers anyway. Even if she left Blueball again.

CHAPTER TWELVE

$\mathcal{R}$ainey

MY SHOULDERS FELL from my ears the second the door closed behind Zeke. He was off to a jobsite that he said couldn't wait another day. Daisy sat at my feet, her tongue just peeking from behind her teeth and her eyes staring at me as if she knew how awkward I'd been all morning and she wanted me to spill my guts to her.

"It's just because we don't know each other that well now," I said on a sigh, pushing around the last of the eggs on my plate that I couldn't eat. Zeke had tried to make breakfast for us again and I'd insisted on doing it instead. I couldn't let him wait on me hand and foot. I wasn't that kind of girl anymore.

Daisy whined.

"What? It has nothing to do with how hot he is now." She huffed out her wet nose. "You know what I'm talking about. Any female would take notice of that physique."

Just the thought of his bare chest, or the look in his deep blue eyes when I did something to make him smile, or even his thick hair that begged for my fingers to run through it...it all made my stomach flip-flop erratically. Perhaps I just needed an antacid and to get a life.

I pushed up from the table and took my plate to the sink. Daisy's nails scratched on the wood floor as she followed me. "I think I'm going to walk into town. Stretch my legs, get a coffee, get out of here." I looked around the house, seeing Zeke everywhere I looked. Yeah, that was what I needed. Some distance. Some time away from the vortex that was Zeke. It didn't take me long to get dressed and say goodbye to Daisy who tried giving me sad eyes.

"I can't take you all the way into town, Dais," I said scratching behind her ears. "I'd have to call Zeke and ask permission and then he'd rush over here to drive me so I didn't have to walk. And the man shouldn't lose out on a job just because I came into his life like a wrecking ball."

It was true. Zeke tended to drop everything where I was concerned. I'd only noticed it now, but looking back through our memories together, I saw that it was a pattern with him. It was... nice. But also disconcerting. No one had ever done that for me before and I wasn't sure what to make of it.

The weather was gorgeous outside with the sun already beating down through the pine trees as I walked. Some peace and quiet in nature broken by the occasional passing car gave me time to think, a luxury I didn't have when I was working two jobs and worried about making rent. I'd worked up a good sweat by the time I made it to the quaint little downtown of Blueball. The shops were brightly painted and flowers were liberally strewn everywhere one could put a pot. The lampposts lining the street were old fashioned but well kept, giving the town a Hallmark Channel vibe. I remembered that Christmastime was even more beautiful here.

"Rainette Shaw?" came a reedy voice from behind me just outside Crazy Beans, the local coffee shop.

I turned to find a little old lady in a pair of cotton capris and matching shirt who looked familiar. She was smiling at me like she knew me. "Yes, that's right."

She clapped her hands and then dug around in her purse before sliding on a pair of thick black-rimmed glasses. Aha! It was Mrs. Moore, one of my English teachers in high school. I saw those glasses in my nightmares a few times when studying for finals way back when.

"It is you!" Mrs. Moore grabbed my shoulders and pulled me in for a hug. When she pulled back, she gave me an up-and-down appraisal that didn't end in disapproval like it always did in high school. "Why, you've grown into a fine young woman, haven't you?"

I lifted a shoulder. "Haven't robbed a bank yet."

Mrs. Moore laughed, the lines deepening on her face. "Oh, Rainette. You were always one of my favorites."

If I'd gotten my coffee already, I would have dropped it. "What?"

Mrs. Moore's eyes sparkled behind those lenses of doom. "You heard me. I had to be hard on you to keep you in line back in high school, but I always admired your spirit. I was sad when you left town, which is why I'm so excited to hear you're back and married to our Zeke. He's a good man."

Her praise made my stomach flip-flop again. "He hasn't robbed a bank either."

Mrs. Moore laughed again, as if I was a damn comedian suddenly. I couldn't remember her so much as smiling, let alone laughing back in high school.

"That's true." She put her hand on my arm. "That man needed a wifey and it absolutely makes sense it's you." Then she was shuffling off down the sidewalk, those thick glasses shoved to the top of her fully gray head.

The guilt was back and this time it had an extra layer of hurt that had more to do with disappointing Zeke. This marriage of convenience was turning out to be anything but convenient.

I yanked on the coffee shop door harder than I should have.

The open sign hanging from the top whacked loudly against the glass, warning of my entrance. Heads swiveled and I tried to paste on a calm smile. Perhaps I should get this coffee to go. Hiding out in Zeke's house was sounding better by the minute. Thankfully, there was no line to order and the guy behind the bar immediately popped his head up from where he was restocking something in the cabinets below the register.

The barista was wider than the doorway I'd just come through and the tattoos all over his exposed tan skin were simply an extra warning. Then he smiled and I felt more at ease.

"What can I get you?"

"How about a caramel latte, iced, please."

"You got it. Swipe there and I'll have it up at the counter in just a few minutes."

I barely got my credit card accepted on the little machine by the register when someone else called my name. Preparing myself for more uncomfortable lying to people I used to know, I made sure my expression wasn't screaming resting bitch face before I turned around.

Four ladies around my age were sitting at a nearby table. The blonde-haired one with shoulders I envied had her hand up, waving me over. Three of them had smiles, but the dark-headed one shot me a scowl that made me nervous.

"Hey," I said lamely, edging closer to their table.

"Rainey, right?" the blonde-haired one asked, not waiting for my confirmation. "I'm Paisley, this is Keva, Audrey, and Marlo."

I tried to remember their names while ignoring the lifted eyebrow from Marlo. "Hi. Sorry for my ignorance, but did we go to school together?"

Audrey, the shortest one, chimed in. "Kinda. We were a few years behind you."

"But we're friends of Zeke," Marlo piped in, her tone not exactly friendly.

"Ah."

Keva hissed something at Marlo I couldn't make out. Paisley ignored the hostile vibes from Marlo. "Want to sit with us?"

I looked over at the counter like a lifeline, but my drink wasn't ready yet. "Well, I was headed home, but I could sit while they make my drink."

Audrey was already up and dragging a chair over. I sat down, making sure I stayed closer to her and not Marlo who flanked my other side.

"Gotta say, we were pretty surprised to hear you two got married," Marlo said accusingly.

"Ignore her," Paisley said. "She's extremely loyal and she worries you'll eat up Zeke and spit him out again."

I nodded, understanding dawning. They were friends of Zeke. He must have told them how I left town. How I hadn't been there for him when his dad died. Suddenly I didn't blame Marlo for not trusting me.

"I understand. Zeke's a good guy."

"Oh, we know that, but do *you* know that?" Marlo snapped.

"Iced caramel latte," the barista announced, sliding the drink on our table and saving me from having to answer Marlo's question.

"Thanks, Lawson," Keva said for me when it's clear I couldn't find my voice. Not after it's so obvious that Marlo didn't like me.

"Any of you ladies looking for a part-time job?" Lawson, the barista, rubbed his hands together. "I need to hire someone as soon as possible."

"Sorry, I'm slammed with work at the clinic," Keva answered.

"Me too," Audrey piped in. "I finally have enough clients I don't have to cut coupons just to afford my weekly groceries."

I opened my mouth to say...something. I couldn't exactly tell them I wasn't staying. Marlo would probably pull out a knife or something. She looked like the type to actually cut a girl, not just threaten it. If I was staying, working at the little coffee shop would be perfect for me. For a quick second, yearning stabbed at my heart. If things were different, staying here in Blueball would be nice.

"Well, spread the word if you can." Lawson knocked his knuckles against the tabletop and then headed back behind the bar. But my eyes felt like they were going to fall right out of their sockets. He had one particular tattoo on his forearm that made my blood run cold.

"See? She can't give me one good reason."

Marlo's sharp voice pulled my thoughts back to the conversation. Paisley put her hand up and argued in my defense, right before all the ladies started talking at once.

The chair scraped loudly against the stamped concrete floor of the coffee shop as I stood up on weak legs.

"I gotta go," I managed to say, snatching my coffee off the table and hustling toward the door.

"See what you did?" I heard Keva admonish Marlo.

Then the door swung shut behind me and I turned right, heading back home as fast as my feet would carry me. By the time I made it to the street that led to Zeke's house, I'd walked off my panic. Pulling my phone from my back pocket, I called Grandma and asked if I could swing by tomorrow to pick up her copy of my father's will. I wanted a chance to read through it one last time before I met with the lawyer. I couldn't have another stipulation come out of the woodwork and prevent me from getting that money.

Tomorrow I'd turn thirty, and I'd be one step closer to independence.

One step closer to leaving my prior life behind.

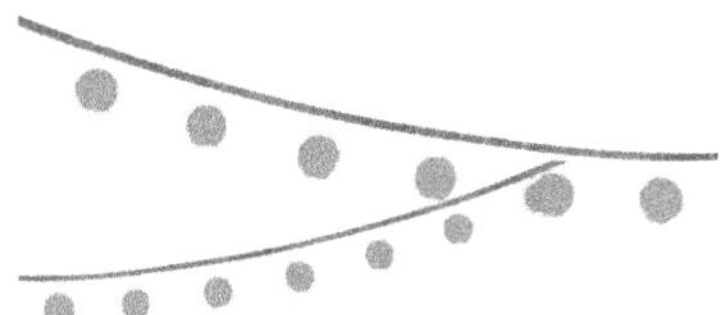

"How'd the shorts work out for you?" Zeke asked, eyeing the fraying edges against my thighs that I'd hacked off last night. My eyes had nowhere to safely land. Not with him walking out of the bathroom without a shirt on again. Jesus. How was a girl supposed to sleep when she had an Adonis lying next to her?

"Good!" I lied.

Zeke cocked his head and studied me. "You're still hot. Here."

He walked over to the doorway of the bedroom and flipped a switch. The overhead fan turned on and kissed my skin with blessed coolness. He'd been so nice to me since he got home from work, but I'd had mostly one-word answers, turning the conversation into awkward silence. I wanted to talk to Zeke. I wanted to tell him everything that had happened since I left Blueball at eighteen, but confiding in him would only make it harder to leave. And I had to leave.

"Thanks," I answered sheepishly.

I had tank tops I could be wearing to bed, but for some reason I felt like these flannel pajamas were the last line of defense. Like if I took them off, there'd be nothing holding me back from climbing on top of my best friend turned husband and begging him to put his hands all over me. God, I was an idiot. I sounded like a bitch in heat, unable to control herself in the presence of a fine male.

Zeke walked up to me, the waistband of his shorts so low I spied that delectable ridge of muscles over his hip bones. I squeezed my eyes shut. If they were going to be traitors and insist on eye-fucking Zeke, then I'd simply close them anytime he was in the room.

His hands swept my hair back from my shoulders and I could feel the heat of him though no other part of us touched. Then his lips were on my forehead, gently placing a kiss there like I was something precious instead of a fucking weirdo with her eyes closed in sawed-off flannel pajamas, shivering at his touch in the middle of summer.

"'Night, Rain," he murmured, stepping back.

I nearly groaned out loud at the loss of his touch. "Night," I croaked, running to the bathroom to use the scissors again to cut off the sleeves of my sleep shirt. Even a late-night sewing session would be better than climbing in that bed with Zeke and begging him to let me curl up in his arms and never let go.

With the bathroom door closed behind me, I blew out a slow breath, trying to calm my heartbeat. I needed to get my shit together. Today's run-in with Lawson at Crazy Beans had been a warning from the universe to not get too comfortable. There were bad people out there and blindly trusting a man seemed to be the lesson I needed to learn in this lifetime.

Message received, universe.

I waited until I thought Zeke might be asleep before creeping out of the bathroom and slipping under the sheets. I made sure I stayed on my side of the bed and not one wayward toe touched him. He might be my husband for another day or two, but touching him would be downright dangerous.

To my future.

And to my heart.

CHAPTER THIRTEEN

eke

THE HIDEOUS ORANGE pancake sizzled in the pan as I flipped it. Rainey had always loved pumpkin pancakes, something that made my stomach turn just thinking about. Pumpkin was a fuckin' vegetable and didn't belong in something as wonderful as a pancake. Don't even get me started on it being in lattes. But it was Rainey's birthday, and what Rainey wanted, Rainey got.

I just hoped she didn't want to leave Blueball today, cash in hand.

She'd been different yesterday. Distant. Like she was in her head about something and I couldn't figure her out. Back when we were teenagers, I'd been able to pick up on her emotions almost as quickly as my own, but grown-up Rainey had me scratching my head. There were too many years between us. Years that had stacked up experiences that didn't include the other person.

Pulling the pancake off the pan, I plated it and topped it with an overwhelming amount of maple syrup and a dollop of whipping cream. I put the plate on a television tray and added a glass of fresh-squeezed orange juice and a red rose from the front yard stuffed in a bud vase. It wasn't gourmet by any means, but it was the best my meager cooking skills could manage without burning the house down.

She was still asleep on her side when I entered the bedroom, the door quietly swinging open when I put my shoulder to it. One hand was on my pillow, showing off the strings that dangled from the ruined sleep shirt. The crazy woman had cut off the arms last night. Her leg was outside of the sheets, as if she'd tried to throw her leg over where my body would have been. That image almost made me bobble the tray. With a steadying breath, I went to my side of the bed and gently put the tray down.

Rainey's eyes fluttered open and I watched in quiet rapture as she blinked up at me in confusion. She was so fuckin' beautiful it made my ribs ache.

"Happy birthday, baby girl," I whispered.

Her lips instantly curved into a grin and everything felt right in my world for the first time since the day before she left Blueball. "You remembered!" Her voice was a croak, but had never sounded lovelier.

"Don't get too excited," I warned, sucking in a deep breath and holding my hand up. I began to sing happy birthday, every single note off-key. Rainey exploded into laughter but clapped along like it was a fuckin' symphony. When I got to the end, she sat up and threw her arms around my neck, rocking the tray of food dangerously. I steadied it while hugging her back.

She pushed away well before I'd gotten my fill of her. Her gaze dropped to the breakfast and her eyes went misty. She covered it up by rearranging the covers so she could sit against the headboard and eat with her legs tucked under. "Jeez, Zeke. How does one not know the words to the happy birthday song? It's literally just one sentence over and over again."

I narrowed my eyes at her, knowing she was teasing me. "Want me to try singing it again and again until I get it right?"

Her gaze flew up to mine, eyes now clear. "Oh, please no."

"Then eat your fuckin' breakfast and be grateful."

She held my gaze with a soft smile. "Thank you."

"You're welcome, Rain." I patted the lump I figured was her leg and then left the room, not trusting myself to stay in her presence any longer without blurting out something that would surely make her run.

Daisy kept whining to get back into the bedroom with Rainey, but I wasn't going to lose my dog to the woman along with my heart. "Come on, girl," I called, pulling open the back door and enticing her with a game of fetch. We played for close to an hour before both of us had burned off our excess energy. When I stepped back inside the house, Rainey was dressed in a pair of jean shorts that hugged her luscious ass and would make a blind man stop to stare.

And just like that, all that frenetic energy was back.

"What would you like to do today?" Rainey asked, bending down to put on her sandals, unaware of the state of my shorts. Daisy's tail whipped my legs before she scrambled across the hardwood to get to Rainey's side. Rainey giggled, fending off her kisses while she got her shoes on and I tried to get myself under control. Was it irrational to be jealous of one's own dog?

"It's your day," I said, voice rough as I looked anywhere but at Rainey and adjusted myself. "But I thought you could take my truck to Crazy Beans and grab us some of that fancy coffee shit you like so much?"

Rainey straightened and I looked back at her, thinking it would be safe with that ass turned the other way. Then I caught sight of her front side in a white tank top with dainty bows tied at the top of her shoulders. Little pink flowers dotted the material. She looked like feminine perfection wrapped in a bow just for me.

"You don't mind me taking your truck?"

I shook my head, trying to make my brain cells work. Pretty

sure all the blood flow in my body was south of the border. "Why would I?"

Rainey shrugged her tan shoulders. "It's just that Danny never let me drive his SUV unless we were on a long trip."

I grimaced at the sound of his name on her lips. Without a working brain to tell me it was a bad idea, I walked over and cupped her face in my hands. She needed to understand how much better she deserved. "Danny was a fuckin' idiot. Men with even a tiny ounce of faith in their woman will let you drive their car."

My words hung in the air between us. Rainey was my woman, always had been. She just didn't know it. Rainey stilled, her eyes searching mine. "You have faith in me?"

"I always have," I answered truthfully. It was her own faith in herself that had been lacking.

Her lips tilted up in a smile, but her eyes stayed sad. And I couldn't bear that sadness in the woman I loved. Especially on her birthday. So I did what I'd been wanting to do since we stood before a judge and promised to love, honor, and cherish each other.

I showed her.

My lips were on hers, and for a heartbeat, I panicked, wondering if she'd push me away. Panic fled the second her hands gripped my forearms and she pulled herself into my chest tighter. Her lips moved, softening, welcoming me. My tongue flicked against her bottom lip and she opened for me, a tiny groan escaping the second I took advantage of the invitation. Her body swayed, all her weight pressing against me as if she instinctively knew I would hold her. The kiss spun out of control, both of us succumbing to an attraction I'd hoped was there but could never confirm until this very moment.

Something lit inside my chest that had nothing to do with the obvious heat between us. This was a flicker of true hope. The first sign that what I felt for Rainey, what I'd always felt, was actually reciprocated.

And so I tore my mouth from hers and let her go, stepping back and watching her sway on her feet. Her eyes flickered open, confusion and lust fighting for dominance. My entire body ached with regret, but I was steadfast. I'd faced the loss of Rainey for twelve fuckin' years. I would not mess this up again. Rainey needed space to figure out what she wanted. If I pushed now, she'd close up on me and run.

So I whistled for Daisy to come over from her doggie bed in the corner of the living room. "I've got a quick job to check on, but we should be back at the same time if you leave now."

"Leave?" Rainey was still in the same spot.

I grinned at the back of her head as I moved to find my keys and wallet. Fighting for Rainey's love was never a game, but it did require strategy. And I had her exactly where I wanted her. Dazed, confused, and wondering if staying in Blueball—with me —was her best option.

"Heads up." I tossed her the keys right as she turned to me. She almost missed them but caught them before they hit the ground.

With a wink and a smile, I left her there, pretending to walk down my driveway. In actuality, I had no job to check in on, but I needed her to leave the house. Daisy stared up at me like I was a dumbass as we hid behind a dense copse of trees just down the road from the house and waited.

"I have a plan, Daisy girl. Just trust me."

I could have sworn she chuffed like a human snort. I heard my truck before I saw it, which stopped me from explaining my entire plan to a dog. There wasn't much of a plan anyway. Rainey made a right turn at the end of the driveway and I waited until the sound of my truck vanished down the road. Then Daisy and I headed back for the house. Pulling my phone out of my pocket, I texted my friends.

Me: The coast is clear.

It didn't take long for my driveway to fill with cars. Paisley, Keva, Audrey, and Marlo filed into the house and out the back door with platters of food and bags of party favors. They barked out orders to me and I complied, appreciating their help even if some of it baffled me. Why did a birthday party need streamers hanging from the trees? That would be a bitch to take down later. Considering I'd never thrown a get-together at my house though, I shut my mouth and did what I was told.

We had very little time to get things set up for a barbecue lunch before Rainey was back. I'd asked Lawson down at Crazy Beans to come up with reasons to keep her there longer, like getting our coffee orders wrong, but knowing Rainey, she might just flip him off and come home without coffee if she got irritated enough.

"Are you sure about all this?" Marlo hissed at me finally. She'd been glaring at me the entire time we got this party set up.

I snapped the lid down on the cooler of beer—not that light piss beer—and tried to allay her fears. When Rainey had come back to town, Marlo had jumped right in to help me, a mark of a true friend I didn't take lightly.

"I know the timing is strange, but you didn't know us back in high school, Marlo. Rainey is it for me. I love her, and I need you to give her a chance."

Marlo looked like chewing rusty nails might be preferable to giving Rainey a chance. She grimaced but nodded her head. "Fine. I'll give her exactly one chance, but don't forget I understand you too, Zeke. We may not have the history but I see you. You love hard and you deserve to be loved hard in return."

Marlo hadn't physically touched me but her words hit like a punch to the gut. She was right, of course. Everyone deserved to be loved, but I also knew something about Rainey that Marlo didn't. Rainey had never been raised in a loving household. Her dad had been indifferent to her, at best. Sure, Gertie had tried to show her love, but Rainey was a temperamental teenager by then who rejected all her attempts at affection. How could I expect

Rainey to love me back when she didn't even know what love was?

I opened my mouth to let her know I appreciated her protectiveness, but the glass slider opened and Gannon, Lincoln, Boston, and Vander piled out onto the back deck. Daisy began to bark her head off, chasing an unsuspecting guest until someone else caught her eye and she bounded over there. Someone started up a speaker with country music flowing at full volume. One of the guys started my barbecue and longneck bottles of beer were passed around. More people started flooding my backyard. In dismay, I tried to catch Paisley's gaze to glare at her, but she stealthily avoided me. I specifically told her to keep the invite list small.

When yet another old teacher of mine slapped me on the back with a congratulations on my marriage, I was already looking for the exit. Wendy, from the courthouse, stood next to my mother, the two talking with their hands more than their mouths. Gertie kept watch by the back slider, which was a good idea. I headed that direction and made it just in time for it to open and a beautiful blonde head to poke out.

The entire crowd shouted happy birthday at Rainey, whose face drained of color. The two iced coffees balanced in one hand began to wobble. The crowd broke into the happy birthday song, sung off-key and at different paces, but the overall energy was upbeat. The last note rang out over the music coming from the speakers and Rainey's face crumbled.

Gertie grabbed the coffees from her hand just in time. Rainey spun on her sandals and ran back inside the house. The crowd went quiet and I held my hand up. Fuck. I never should have let this thing get out of hand like this. I knew she wouldn't want the whole town here.

"She's okay. Just overwhelmed. Keep eating. I'll go get her."

Then I raced inside to rescue the birthday girl.

CHAPTER FOURTEEN

ainey

I MADE it all the way to Zeke's bedroom before the first tear slid down my cheek. If a hole had magically opened up at my feet, offering safe passage to a deserted island, I would have gladly jumped in. All those people. Staring at me. Singing. Wishing me happy birthday. I groaned and sank down onto the bed, my face resting in my shaky hands.

Being the center of attention had been fun when I was a teenager. Being wild and reckless had soothed the hurt my father had created when he ignored me all those years. But somehow, being an adult, trying to scrape by with multiple jobs and rent coming due and grocery bills getting steeper and run-ins with assholes had made me retreat to the safety of the shadows. Being one tiny fish in a sea of bigger fish had suited me just fine in the city. I no longer even liked being the center of attention.

What made it worse was seeing the faces of all the people who'd welcomed me with open arms years ago. They'd accepted me. Showed me what community actually looked like. And what had I done? Tore out of here the first chance I got, thinking I could do better. Thinking *I* was better.

I was such a dumbass.

"Rain?" Zeke's gentle voice came from the doorway.

I couldn't lift my head and look him in the eye. His attention was worse than everyone else's. As a child, I'd learned to ignore my father's negligent behavior as a surviving mechanism. In high school I'd continued doing the same, not knowing any other way to live. I'd ignored Zeke's efforts to love me. Now to add insult to injury, he'd bent over backwards for me since I'd been back, but the truth was painfully obvious despite everything he did: I wasn't worthy of anyone's attention.

The mattress dipped as Zeke sat beside me, his big hand coming up to rub circles on my back. I cringed inside. Not from his touch. God, no, not from his touch. I wanted to curl into his side and let him continue to fight my battles for me. I cringed because I didn't deserve his kindness. He'd thrown a birthday party for me after serving me breakfast in bed and I'd ruined that too.

"What's going on in that head of yours?" he finally asked.

"Why did you do this?" I asked, voice muffled as it traveled through my hands.

"The party?" Zeke's hand stopped circling my back but he didn't take it off me. "To be honest, I shouldn't have."

My heart cracked even as he gave voice to the same conclusion I'd come to. Even he knew I wasn't worthy of a party.

"I shouldn't have tried to manipulate you like that," Zeke went on. "I thought if you could see how much everyone was glad to have you back home, you'd stay longer."

I lifted my head, thoroughly confused. The line between Zeke's eyebrows softened as he took in my watery eyes and wet cheeks. He lifted his hand off my back, and instead of getting up and announcing he'd tell everyone to leave, he pulled me into his arms and tucked me against his chest.

"Why are you crying?" he asked gently, the rumble of his voice vibrating against my ear.

I inhaled slowly, my eyes closing. There was nowhere else I'd rather be. Ever. What did that say about me that my best friend had become the only refuge I'd ever known? Was that normal? Was I confusing friendship with sexual attraction? Because that kiss this morning had made my toes curl. Definitely not in a friendly way.

"Rain?" he prompted when I took too long to answer.

I sniffled, hoping I wouldn't get snot and tears all over his shirt. "I don't deserve a party."

Zeke inhaled sharply, his arms turning to steel bands around my torso. His growl had my eyes widening. "Who the fuck told you that?"

"Um, me?" I pushed off his chest, knowing I looked terrible but I needed him to understand. "I left this town like I was too good for it, Zeke. Now I'm back, twelve years later with my tail between my legs, and I'm supposed to believe that everyone out there is happy to throw me a birthday party?"

Zeke looked like he was going to crush something by sheer force of will. "Yes."

I scoffed. "Zeke. Seriously."

"I am being serious. Everyone—well, everyone except Marlo, who doesn't trust anyone unless they're dead—is very happy to throw you a party."

"Why?" I asked incredulously. That made zero sense. I'd offended everyone when I left town and hurt Zeke. I'd abandoned my grandma. I was kind of an awful person back when I was a teenager.

Zeke shrugged. "Because Blueball is different. Those people out there genuinely want to know you. The grown-up Rainey Shaw. We don't hold things against people forever. People make mistakes. But you have to put in the effort this time around if you want to make things right. Allow yourself to have friends, Rain."

The panic was back and so were the tears filling my eyes and making everything in my vision shimmer. "I don't know how to do that."

"Bullshit," Zeke fired back. "You and I were best friends once. And I'm not exactly easy to be friends with. You know how."

I picked at the comforter underneath me, trying to pinpoint why my heart was racing. "Feels like making friends is dangerous."

"Why?

I shrugged. "Well, I never stay in one place very long, so it seems kind of pointless."

Zeke tilted his head. "I call bullshit again. You can live in another country and still keep up friendships. There are these things called smartphones."

I smacked his knee but he kept right on going.

"I think you're afraid of letting anyone get close to you. You think we're all going to let you down like your father did."

My breath froze in my lungs. Zeke grabbed my hands and held them tight. "You think you're not worthy of a birthday party, not worthy of friends, because of how your father treated you. Am I close?"

My eyes slid shut and I blew out a shaky breath. "I thought you were a builder, not a psychologist," I teased, the joke falling flat.

"Do you want to make friends, Rainey?"

I opened my eyes and stared at the one person in my life who'd always been there for me, even when I hadn't been there for him. "Yes."

And oh how I meant it. I desperately wanted friends. I'd spent the last twelve years lonely, searching for more out of life when I'd left all that mattered to me back in this little town.

"Then get your gorgeous ass outside and fake it 'til you make it. That's what I do in social situations, a skill a certain someone taught me." Zeke winked and I knew he was referring to me and my very awesome advice from our freshman year of high school.

I slid one of my hands away from his and wiped at my face. "There is one thing I know how to do."

Zeke grunted.

"I know how to party."

That earned me a rare grin from Zeke. "Yeah, wife, you do know how to party." He shook his head, probably remembering all the times he held my hair back as I puked up Four Loko, my drink of choice back then. "Come party with me."

That was an offer I couldn't refuse. Not anymore.

Zeke slid off the bed and held his hand out for me. I took it, rising and following him back outside where I hoped no one could see my red eyes. Thankfully, I was no longer the center of attention. Everyone was in groups, talking, eating, and drinking. They included me whenever Zeke dragged me with him, the two of us being as social as we knew how to be. Daisy kept to my side until some of the little kids belonging to Zeke's friends dognapped her with a bag of treats, settling into the living room to watch a movie.

Eventually, the beer turned to mixed drinks and my blood alcohol level got just high enough that I loosened up. Most of the older crowd went home to make Sunday dinner. The boys cranked up the volume on the speakers that promised angry letters from Zeke's neighbors tomorrow. My eyes lit up when one of my favorite songs came on.

"Dance with me!" I shouted up to Zeke. He groaned, but let me drag him over to the little patch of grass next to the back deck where other couples were dancing.

His arms came around my waist and my hands snuck into the hair on the back of his head. My breasts were smashed against his stomach, not a single centimeter of air between us. My skin held a light sheen of sweat from the hot afternoon sun. I tipped my head back, eyes closed, and just grinned up at the sky. I really was having fun.

Zeke dipped his head and skimmed his nose up the column of my throat. I gasped, my head coming back up to stare at him just an inch away from my face.

"Happy looks good on you," he said gruffly, gaze drifting down my body to where we're smashed together.

My head felt like it was going to float right off my body. There it was again, that tingle of awareness that hadn't left me since he kissed me this morning. I couldn't catch my breath and I wasn't sure if that was from him or from the dancing. Our hips moved together, a subtle rocking motion that wasn't even with the beat of the music at this point.

"I think *you* look good on me," I said back, staring at his mouth. If the birthday girl was given one wish on her day, mine was that those lips would be on my skin. Right. Freaking. Now.

Apparently old, impulsive Rainey hadn't completely left me because next thing I knew, I tugged on his neck, bending him down even further. As soon as he was in range, I pressed my lips to his and took what I wanted. His answering groan, right before he hauled me off the ground and took the kiss from the slow lane to the fast lane, told me he wanted this too. His tongue dipped inside and everything perfect about our wedding kiss was amplified here in his backyard.

A wolf whistle broke through our awareness, breaking us apart on a gasp. I swallowed hard, realizing I'd wrapped a leg around Zeke's waist, as if I had plans to climb him like a freaking tree while we kissed. I dropped my leg and also my face, resting my forehead against his chest. I wasn't sweating because of the afternoon heat any longer. A bead of sweat dripped down my spine from straight embarrassment. How many people just saw us making out at my birthday party?

The low vibration coming off Zeke's chest had me glancing up, thinking he was angry. Instead, I found him smiling ear to ear, looking down at me like I amused him. He tucked a lock of hair behind my ear before I realized he was laughing.

"Why are you laughing?" I hissed as quietly as I could, aware of all the heads turned in our direction.

He swayed to the side again, as if we hadn't missed a beat with our out-of-control kiss. All the blood drained from my brain when I felt how hard he was behind those jeans that fit him just right. Holy shit. Zeke kept dancing as if this wasn't a giant turning point in our friendship.

"I've been waiting for you to do that for sixteen long years." His lopsided grin made the edges of my mouth turn up, such was the power of his smile. "It was every bit as wonderful as I dreamed it would be."

And then he kissed my forehead and kept dancing like this was suddenly our own personal *Dirty Dancing* dance floor, clearly as turned on as I was and not doing a damn thing to stop it. His hips rocked against mine and every slumbering cell that had put my libido on the back burner the last few years woke up all at once. My skin was on fire and my nipples felt every shift against his body as if there were no clothes between us. I dropped my forehead to his chest again and held on for dear life.

I didn't know if it was the alcohol flowing through my veins or simply the culmination of the temptation building between us over the last few days, but I wanted every single one of these people at Zeke's house to go home.

Right freaking now.

CHAPTER FIFTEEN

eke

IF THERE WAS one thing I could say I was good at, it would be holding back. I'd held my tongue for four years around Rainey, stuffing down my true feelings and being the friend she needed at the time. Dad died and I stuffed down those feelings too. They were too big, too overwhelming to address when my heart was already bruised from Rainey leaving me behind. I held back every time the girls tried to force me to make friends, knowing I had zero capacity to give myself to a friendship that would probably just blow up in my face. And now that Rainey was here in Blueball this time around, I'd been holding back yet again, showing her I loved her with my actions, but keeping myself leashed so as not to scare her away.

But then she kissed me. She. Kissed. *Me.*

And I was fuckin' done holding back.

I knew she could feel me. Feel how hard she made me as she pranced around in those tiny shorts, her long blonde hair flicking against her lightly tanned shoulders and back. Her eyes had gone wide, but she hadn't pulled away. I ground against her stomach, letting her feel every inch of me that wanted her. Her eyelids fluttered closed and the heat in her cheeks wasn't all due to the setting sun. Her tongue darted out to wet her lips and I nearly lost all control right there in front of the town I grew up in.

The music turned down and Gannon clapped me on the shoulder. I blinked, lifting my head and seeing that most everyone had gone home. Only Audrey and Boston remained on the makeshift dance floor with us. Boston clearly had the same thought I did: how could I get my woman naked and under me in the next three minutes?

And make no mistake, Rainey was my woman. Not because of the marriage license we both signed either. I might not get her naked like I wanted, but we sure as hell were going to get some things straight between us tonight.

"Go tell the girls goodbye and then meet me inside," I murmured against Rainey's forehead before kissing her there. I forced my hands to let go of her. To step away and turn my back on her. I couldn't just throw her on the ground and have my way with her like an animal in heat, no matter how badly I wanted to.

"Thanks for cleaning up," I told Gannon, seeing how he and Paisley had gathered all the trash in some bags and put away the leftover food.

He pulled his baseball hat off his head and put it back on backwards, waggling his eyebrows at me. "You were a little preoccupied."

"Fuck off," I blustered, knowing he had every right to tease me. I practically made out with Rainey right there in the middle of her birthday party.

"I hope we both get to fuck off tonight, my friend."

I cracked a grin at his crude joke and said goodbye to the rest of the folks remaining. Before long, the backyard was empty, save Daisy who was hoovering the grass for dropped hot dogs and chips. I whistled and she bounded over, her tongue hanging out the side of her snout. Clearly she had a good time at this party too. We stepped inside the glass slider and saw that the living room had been cleared of kids, but blankets and bowls of snacks remained. I'd have to clean that up tomorrow. Right now, I had a wife to find.

"Rainey?" I called out, hoping she hadn't just tipped right into bed and fallen asleep while I was cleaning things out back. I knew she'd had a few drinks, but all my plans for the night would be ruined if she'd had too many to have a conversation.

Music coming from my bedroom suddenly turned on and my head swiveled toward the hallway. A song played that I recognized, but couldn't place. Daisy stayed by my side as we walked down the hallway to my bedroom door. Anticipation built and the usual voice in my head told me not to get my hopes up. I told that asshole to shut the fuck up. Tonight was not about holding back any longer.

As I hit the doorway, I saw Rainey standing with her back to me, her head swiveled so she could shoot me a saucy look over her shoulder. She lifted a hand and pulled at the string on her shoulder, untying one of the bows that held her top up. I stepped into the room and shut the door behind me, keeping Daisy out. I loved the girl but not even she could keep me from what I hoped was about to happen in this room.

Familiar lyrics sang out from wherever Rainey had stashed her phone and she mouthed the words at me over her shoulder, starting with "oh, lover boy." I realize it's a song from *Dirty Dancing*, the movie she made me watch with her before every homecoming dance. Then her hips began to shimmy and I nearly choked on my own spit, drawn right back to the present. Every hope, every dream I'd ever had about her was coming true right before my eyes.

She pulled the string on the other shoulder and her top fell to her hips, leaving her back bare. Another shake of her hips and her hands unsnapped the button of her jean shorts. A few beats later, as I slowly died inside waiting, she shimmied out of the shorts, letting all the material drop to her bare feet.

Rainey Shaw was finally, gloriously naked in my bedroom.

I sucked in a deep breath, admiring the shape of her legs, the flare of her hips, and the tuck of her waist. She had small tattoos dotting the ridge of her spine where I could see them without the curtain of her hair, symbols I wanted to study and understand. But then she spun around, gifting me with the naked view of her front side. Breasts so beautiful and round I could have wept stared back at me. Dusky nipples pebbled under my gaze. I groaned, not sure how much perfection a man could look at without falling to his knees.

Rainey's eyes were wide as my gaze finally lifted to hers. She was nervous. Even as she boldly stripped for me, there was a part of her that was nervous I'd reject her. She didn't understand that rejecting her was something I simply could not do. It was like asking ice to not be cold. Or leaves to not turn color in the fall. Simply impossible.

So I gave her what she needed. The acceptance she craved as much as she would deny it. I stripped my shirt over my head and threw it on top of her clothes. Her eyes immediately dropped to my chest, want replacing the nerves. Toeing my shoes off, I snapped my belt free of my jeans. A flirtatious grin slipped back onto her face. Shoving the jeans down, I kicked them aside, standing before her perfectly naked, just like her. If vulnerable was how she was feeling, I'd meet her there.

"You're...stunning," I managed to say, the words slipping across the distance between us. Anything I could say would be inadequate, but she deserved the best words I could find. "Perfect."

Her head bowed, and when she lifted it again, her lip was caught against her teeth. "I want you, Zeke."

My eyes slid shut for a split second, savoring the very thing I'd been wanting to hear for years, knowing I'd be playing it on repeat in my head for years to come. My cock, already hard and ready to go the second Rainey had kissed me an hour ago, engorged further.

"And I want you." That was the understatement of the year.

I crossed the room, watching as her gaze dipped to take in all of me. When I stood right in front of her, my dick almost touching her soft skin, her gaze flew back to my face. The nerves were back.

"I don't…"

I cupped her face with one hand, making her hold my gaze. "You don't want what, Rainey? Say it so I know what you need."

I felt her throat bunch as she swallowed. "I don't want to ruin our friendship."

"Then we won't. What else?"

Her eyes pleaded with me. As if I'd let anything come between us ever again. I nodded firmly at her, to let her know that I was serious. Nothing would hinder our friendship. Not twelve years apart. And certainly not sex. It looked like she believed me.

"Then fuck me, Zeke," she whispered, stepping into my body and slipping her hands up to the back of my neck. She kissed the center of my chest, the highest she could reach without me bending down. Just the feel of her lips against my skin made me feel out of control.

I would do anything for Rainey, and had the marriage license to prove it, but I couldn't do that. Not yet. Not now. Not our first time.

Instead, I reached down and slid my arm under her legs, hauling her against my chest and carrying her over to my side of the bed. I laid her down carefully, then stood back to look my fill. She had another tattoo on her left hip. A flock of birds in flight. My index finger traced them all, my mouth following as I bent over her. I knew what they symbolized. Rainey was those birds, needing to fly free. It would only spell heartbreak for me, but I was selfish enough, desperate enough, that I'd take this time with her now. I'd take whatever she could give me. Even if it was never enough.

"Zeke," Rainey gasped as I flicked my tongue against the skin at her hip. Her hands slid into my hair and gripped hard.

"Shh," I murmured against her skin, sliding my hands over her hips and down her soft thighs. Fuck, she was small. But I knew better than to think she was fragile. Rainey was a mighty powerhouse in a small package. And I was going to take my time, tasting every single inch of her.

I stood straight and came around to the foot of the bed, my hands reaching for her feet. Her toenails were painted bright pink and a thin gold chain surrounded one ankle. I bent, kissed the ankle, and trailed my lips up first one leg, then the other. Her smooth skin felt like silk under my fingertips.

"Zeke, please," Rainey begged, her head already twisting left and right on my pillow.

"Shh." I would not rush this.

When I got to her knees, I gripped her thighs and slowly spread them apart. Rainey's breaths began to come in pants, her chest rising and falling rapidly. But she let me open her to my gaze, her pink center already wet and ready for me. Something wrapped around my chest and didn't let go, telling me I was the luckiest bastard in the whole world to have this woman trust me.

I crawled onto the bed and used my shoulders to spread her legs wider, ignoring her aimless pleas. Rainey wanted more, and she'd get more. When I was good and ready. I dipped my head and kissed the inside of each thigh, taking a moment to let her scent wrap around me. Memorizing it. Filing it away in case she left me again. She lifted her hips, chasing my face, and I held her back down with my palm on the center of her belly.

"Greedy, little Rain," I growled.

"Please, Zeke. Stop teasing me." She lifted her head off the pillow to shoot me a dirty look that had no heat behind it. Her eyes were already dazed and I hadn't even gotten to the best part.

"I'm not teasing you." I was making love to her, a distinction she would absolutely hate. And one I wasn't willing to compromise on.

I dipped my head and ran my tongue from bottom to top, smiling against her flesh when she keened loudly, dropping her head back to the pillow. Her taste bloomed on my tongue and I dove back in, a starved man finally being fed. I thrust my tongue inside of her and then back out. Grazed my teeth against her clit and then sucked it into my mouth. Her cries were music to my ears, drowning out the songs coming from her phone. I slid a single finger inside her slick heat and barely paid her clit any attention before she tightened around me and shattered, trembling all over and chanting my name. I grinned, taking my time to ease her down, feeling like I could stay right here all night.

Her hands finally tightened on my hair, pulling me away from her. "Enough!" She giggled, though it turned into a moan again as I slipped my finger out of her. "Please, Zeke."

I climbed over her and lay fully on top of her body, keeping most of my weight in my elbows on either side of her head. "Please what?" I dipped my head and kissed her, the quick peck I intended quickly burning out of control as she dipped her tongue inside my mouth. Fuck, I loved kissing Rainey.

Her fingernails bit into my ass and I broke away from her lips with a yelp. Her triumphant grin only made me harder. Her voice was all candy and honey, dripping with the feminine wile only she could pull off. "Fuck me, please."

A low growl came from my chest. She made it very hard to deny her. Especially when part of me wanted exactly what she was begging for. I pushed away from her and leaned over to the bedside table, pulling out a condom from the drawer. I sheathed myself as she watched, her eyelids heavy, that tongue darting out to lick her lips. She reached for me and I lay back over her, spreading her thighs once again. Notching myself against her, I paused, staring deep into her eyes.

"You're sure?" She probably thought I meant the fucking. What I actually meant was something way deeper. If we did this, she was mine. Not because of a fuckin' piece of paper from the courthouse. She was mine. Forever. Here or long distance.

She nodded, wrapping her leg around my waist and holding on to my neck. I slid one glorious inch inside of her tight heat and nearly came on the spot. Teenage me would have and I thanked my lucky stars for this moment when I was a grown-ass adult and could wrangle some semblance of control.

"Please, Zeke," Rainey begged again, lifting her hips and letting another inch of me inside of her. A moment later, she tried the same move again, but I stopped her, spreading her knees wide and taking away her control. I was going to enjoy every fuckin' second of this and she wasn't going to rush me.

I pulled back and then plunged back in, a little further this time. Rainey squeezed her eyes shut and let out that high-pitched, soft keen that tore me apart. Letting go of her knees, I held her face, my grip not as gentle as I would have liked had I had my full control available. Her eyes flew open in surprise.

"Just like that. Eyes on me, baby girl." I slid in further, rewarding her. Her eyes fluttered, but she held my gaze. Pulling back once more, I gave in and thrust all the way to the hilt this time. She gasped, breathing hard and pulsing around me. I stilled, goose bumps lining every inch of my skin.

"Fuck, you feel good," I mumbled.

Rainey tried to lift her hips again, urging me to move faster, but I wouldn't let her, pinning her to the bed and going at my own leisurely pace. I pulled out and then plunged back in, the feel of her so luxurious and right I was pretty sure I could do this all night long. Again and again until both of us couldn't possibly move.

But the feel of her tightening around me with every lazy thrust had me grasping for control and not finding it. Every moan, every keen, every time her hands roamed to a new part of me she hadn't touched before, I lost more of that control. I felt the moment her muscles sputtered around me. Her body froze and her eyes widened and she tilted her head back, finally breaking the deep gaze we'd been locked in.

She cried out long and loudly, her whole body trembling as she shattered. I looked down at her, dropping south to see where we were joined and that last thread of control was yanked from my hands. Lightning struck my spine and my body went rigid. Time stood still and pleasure treaded the line of pain. Her quakes became mine, and in all ways that mattered, we were one as we both fell over the edge together.

CHAPTER SIXTEEN

ainey

I USED to scoff at people who said they had a moment of clarity, an epiphany, if you will. Something that changed the trajectory of their life. It sounded as hokey and pie in the sky as saying soul mates were a thing. The school of hard knocks had taught me that life was merely what you make it. You want something, you work for it. Strikes of brilliance or the waving of a magic wand were strictly for fairy tales.

But as I looked up into Zeke's face, his jaw hard but his eyes soft, his body moving in me, over me, through me, making love to me when I was fighting his love tooth and nail...well, I felt it. That moment where all your life experiences coalesce into one shining example of the only truth that makes any kind of sense.

This man was the person I'd been missing all my life.

And as I tipped over the edge and he came with me, because that was all he'd ever been trying to do since I'd known him—be right by my side—a whole new world unlocked inside of me. That sacred trust I'd given to no one after my father abused me of the notion, was somehow pulsing with life again. The love I'd deflected out of fear was battering at the walls I'd put up to protect myself.

Zeke didn't say a word as we both lay there catching our breaths, but he didn't have to. He'd been telling me over and over again how he felt about me. I just hadn't been listening. Hadn't opened myself to the possibility of trusting someone else to the depth that I knew he wanted. The way he deserved. So as he bundled me into his arms and kissed the back of my head, slowly drifting into sleep, I lay there, wide awake, tears slipping down my cheeks and soaking the pillow.

I saw every hour on the bedside clock, catching a few minutes of sleep here and there, but fully awake when the pitch blackness of night began to ease. I slipped out of Zeke's arms and froze on the side of the bed until his breathing settled again. My thighs were deliciously sore as I silently stood, my body unused to being shared with someone else.

I didn't allow myself to look down at Zeke, knowing I wouldn't be able to do what I needed to if I saw his beautiful face. On tiptoe, I snuck around the room, grabbing articles of clothing I hoped were mine before patting Daisy's head when it lifted and hoping she wouldn't give me away. I dressed in the hallway and grabbed my wallet off the kitchen table. Sandals would have to wait until I got outside so as not to make any noise.

There was a chill in the air that I knew would fade quickly as the sun rose in the sky. My steps were quick, but my heart was heavy. Everything was more unsettled than before Zeke and I had sex. A temporary marriage was one thing, but consummating it? Even I was not dumb enough to think that hadn't changed things. And I didn't mean legally.

The downtown area of Blueball wasn't quite awake when I got to the bank on foot. A few people were hustling from their cars to their shops, unlocking doors and turning on lights. I sat on the bench outside the bank and watched the town come to life. I heard movement behind the window and I turned to see an aging teller getting the bank ready. Right on time, the woman unlocked the door and opened it, smiling warmly at me.

"Good morning. Come on in. I'll be with you in a moment."

"Thanks." I headed inside and shifted my weight from foot to foot until she reappeared behind the secure plexiglass and waved me up.

"What can I help you with, hon?"

"I'd like to transfer a lump sum from a trust account?" The lawyer I'd spoken with just days ago assured me that everything was done on their end, but I wouldn't believe it until the money was officially transferred into my account.

"Sure. Do you have the trust agreement and your identification?"

I pulled both items out of my purse and slid them through the slot. She clicked away on the computer for a bit and then asked me to swipe my debit card for the account I wanted the money transferred to. My hands shook, but I did as she requested, and not more than two minutes later, just shy of one million dollars was sitting in my checking account. The account that dipped below zero almost every other month as I tried to make ends meet.

"All done. Anything else I can help you with today?" The woman was smiling at me. I felt like I might pass out from relief.

"That's it. Thank you so much."

I turned and left, tucking my driver's license back into my purse. The sun had already turned the air warm outside as I exited the bank, now a much richer woman than when I'd walked in. I turned left and right, unsure where to go. When I'd dreamed of this moment of freedom, I always thought I'd be dancing in the street, or shoving my fist in the air, or whooping my way to the next town I wanted to explore. Reality was quite different.

Instead of doing any of those things, I headed toward the park, sagging onto a bench in the middle of the grassy field under an old oak tree. I carefully avoided looking at the bridge. I couldn't look at our spot and think clearly, and boy, did I need to be thinking clearly right now. There were important decisions to be made now that the entire world lay at my feet. I had options. So many freaking options.

On the one hand, I could leave town just like I'd planned. And I wanted to. Badly. The itch to run when things got heated was driving me mad. But then I pictured Zeke singing as he presented me with pumpkin pancakes. Or Daisy tackling us as we sat out in his yard and just talked. Or the way he'd touched me last night, so careful, so reverent.

I sucked in a deep breath and looked up at the leaves shimmering in the early morning breeze. I'd hurt him once and I refused to do it again. No matter how uncomfortable it made me to stay in one spot and work things out, I wouldn't hurt Zeke again.

"No iced coffee this morning?"

The voice right behind the bench startled me. I jumped, nearly falling off my wooden seat as I spun around. Lawson, the barista from Crazy Beans, held up his hands.

"Whoa. Sorry. Didn't mean to startle you. I called your name." He moved in front of me but kept his distance.

I put my hand to my chest and tried to breathe. There were people out now. Not many, but enough that I could scream and get attention. I'd learned some self-defense over the years, so I wasn't scared. But I was alert.

His head tilted and then his mouth opened and closed as his eyes went wide. "I thought you looked familiar."

"Excuse me?"

He rubbed a hand over the scruff on his jaw. Then he bared his forearm to me, pointing to the tattoo I'd seen that first day in his shop. The one that struck fear in my heart.

"I was there that night. Took me a second to figure out why I knew you. You were Hawk's girl, right?"

Now I was officially scared.

I shook my head, gaze darting around to assess my exits. The town gym was the closest building. Lawson looked incredibly strong, but odds were good I could outrun him.

"I was never Hawk's girl." The words came out sharper than I intended.

"Hey. Sorry. I'm going about this wrong." Lawson put his hands up again. "I'm no longer with them. One stint in prison was all I needed to get my shit straight. I have nothing to do with that club, I promise you."

I eyed him warily, looking for a lie. He looked like he was telling the truth, but then again, I'd been a stupid girl trusting Hawk all those years ago. My judgement didn't exactly have a strong record.

"Listen, I don't exactly go around telling people about my history. I don't lie about it if someone asks directly, but you wouldn't believe how hard it is to get a job after you've been in prison. It's why I opened my own shop. I'm my own boss and I keep my nose clean." Lawson's gaze turned to one of pity. "Did you get out okay?"

He was referring to a time I tried to never think about. My eyes glazed over with hot tears. Seconds ticked by with neither one of us speaking. Lawson finally nodded and turned to go.

"I was only eighteen."

His gaze snapped up to mine. "I figured. They liked younger girls."

I nodded. "I was so dumb. I hopped on his bike and zoomed out of here like I had any idea of what I was doing."

"That's what they count on. They're bullies, preying on naive girls and running drugs to make a living." Lawson took a tentative step closer. "Did you hear they were all arrested?"

I shook my head. "No." As soon as I'd left, only two weeks after ditching Blueball, I hitchhiked myself as far away as I could. Buried my head in work and made a life for myself, trying to forget those two weeks with Hawk.

"May I?" Lawson gestured to the seat next to me on the bench.

I nodded and he sat, running his hands against his jeans nervously.

"I helped take them all down, as part of my plea bargain, but I still feel guilty for not doing something about the women. I'm sorry I didn't help you get out."

I shot him a soft smile. "You didn't know me."

He shrugged. "Still should have helped."

We sat there and chatted about those times, filling in holes and sharing our nightmares. It was cathartic somehow, talking about the two weeks I wished never happened. It was the darkest part of my life, but without it, I wouldn't have grown up. Wouldn't have become the woman I was today. By the time Lawson said he had to get to work, we were laughing together. I knew I'd made a friend.

"Thank you," I whispered.

"For what?"

"For being a good guy."

Lawson looked haunted by that statement. "I wasn't always, but I'm trying to be now." He patted my knee. "I'm glad you're back, Rainey. Blueball is a hell of a town."

I grinned, knowing exactly what he meant. The place grew on you. The people ensnared you with their kindness. "I'm glad I'm back too."

"What the hell, Rain?"

Zeke's angry grumble had both of us spinning to the right to see Zeke standing there with his arms crossed over his chest. His clothes were wrinkled and his hair looked like he'd stuck his hand on a live wire.

Lawson jumped off the bench and held his hands up again. "I think it's time I got to work."

"That's a real fuckin' good idea."

"Zeke!"

Zeke shot me a look so full of hurt and anger I snapped my mouth shut.

"It's okay. Nice to chat with you, Rainey. See you around."

"You too, Lawson."

Zeke glared at me while Lawson walked away. I wasn't sure what he was so pissed about. I'd actually never seen him look at me that way before. I opened my mouth to wish him a good morning, but he beat me to it, his voice punishing with his insinuation.

"That looked cozy."

eke

I KNEW my anger was over the top and directed at the wrong person. Lawson hadn't done anything wrong, exactly. He was, however, looking way too fuckin' cozy with my wife, considering he, like everyone else, thought our marriage was real. There were tears in Rainey's eyes as I stalked up to them, and I was jealous another man had gotten to comfort her.

When I woke up this morning and she was nowhere to be found, I'd been scared. Angry. Bitter that I'd given the same woman my heart again, only to be left in the dust. It was fuckin' groundhog day. When I saw her on the bench in the park as I was on my way to our spot to find her, I was both relieved to see she was still in Blueball, and pissed she'd been talking so intimately with Lawson when I wanted to be everything to her. Maybe last night had only been sex to Rainey, but it had been yet another declaration of my love.

And fuck me for being willing to offer her my body before I'd gotten a chance to reel in her heart.

"Are you kidding me right now?" Rainey snapped, standing up from the park bench and squaring off with me.

I fuckin' loved that too. Her spirit. The way she didn't fear me in the least.

Her purse slid down her arm and she pulled the strap back over her shoulder. My gaze snagged on the folded white papers sticking out of the leather. Clarity hit like a lightning bolt.

"You were leaving again," I whispered. Not a question. A statement of truth. She went to the bank and got her money. I was no longer of use to her.

With a blow to the chest that stole my breath, I spun on my heel and marched away. Vaguely I heard Rainey call my name, but I was too pissed—and yeah, fuckin' *hurt*—to turn around. I'd been playing the long game again, showing Rainey how much I loved her while she'd been planning her quick exit.

Two hands grabbed my elbow and wrenched me around. Rainey was breathing hard and snapping electricity from her eyeballs as she glared me down. Those same hands came up to my chest and she shoved me backward. My shoulder blades and skull cracked against something hard. The bridge. We were right by our spot, though the wildflowers didn't pervade my space with peace and calm like they normally did.

"Quit running away!"

I gaped at her. "Oh, that's rich. Rainey Shaw telling *me* not to run away."

Hurt crept into those angry eyes. "Low blow, Zeke."

I pointed at her purse that was now dragging along the ground. "Isn't that what you're doing? Running away again? Got your money, so fuck everyone else, right?"

Rainey's eyes filled with tears, even as her chest pumped air in and out in a rapid pace. "Yes, I got my money. No, I wasn't leaving town." Her gaze skittered away and my lungs felt crushed. "I thought about it."

I straightened my spine and tried to shift out of her way, but she jumped in front of me, her chest plowing into my torso. "I thought about it, but I couldn't bear to hurt you again," she said, emphasizing every word.

It wasn't a declaration of love—not by a long shot—but it was something. And I wasn't too proud to grasp at straws if it meant I got Rainey's heart in the long term.

Grasping her by the arms, I spun us around and pressed her into the side of the bridge, her inhales rubbing her chest against me, a constant distraction. Gritting my teeth together so hard I feared my molars would crack, I asked her a simple question.

"Why not? You did it before, why not do it again?"

Her eyes darted left and right, searching mine for something I couldn't provide her. She had to figure this out on her own. Her cheeks went from pink to red, matching the leftover tears in her eyes.

"Because I care about you, all right!" she shouted. "And I wasn't cuddled up with Lawson, you big dummy. He was listening to me talk because I was crying."

My heart melded a few of its pieces back together again as she declared she cared about me. It was paltry in comparison to the love I felt for her, but I was a desperate man. Always had been where it concerned Rainey. Ignoring her first statement to address the more pressing issue, I vowed silently to come back to the first.

"Why were you crying? Are you hurt?" I ran my hands up and down her arms, checking her person for injury, but she seemed fine. Overwhelmed emotionally, for sure, but not physically harmed.

Rainey lifted her nose in the air, her eyes shifting to a steely blue that always came before she said something that would certainly piss me off. "No, I'm not hurt. But I was."

Her words hung there for a long moment as I tried to under-stand. When it still didn't make sense, she sighed, grabbed my hands off her arms and tugged me to the bench I'd made for our spot, pulling me down to sit next to her. She didn't let go of my hands, but her knee was bobbing up and down, giving away her nervousness.

"It's a long story. You sure you want to hear it?"

"I want to know everything about you," I answered easily, because it was the truth.

"Do you remember the day I left Blueball?"

My jaw hardened. "In excruciating detail, yes."

Her hand tightened on mine. "I was so excited to have an adventure with Hawk. He and I had been messaging for weeks before graduation."

I squeezed my eyes shut, wondering if maybe I didn't want to hear this story after all. It would only hurt me more. Then again, it might help me understand Rainey. If I could understand why she left, maybe I could provide what she needed so she didn't feel like she had to leave again.

"He picked me up and the ride on the back of his Harley was exhilarating. We stopped at a lookout point and he had a flask on him. We took turns sipping and talking. He invited me back to his place, though he didn't specify where he lived. I agreed." Rainey stopped and sighed, her shoulders sagging. "I was such an idiot."

"You were barely eighteen and probably drunk." While I agreed with her assessment, I wasn't going to let Hawk off the hook. He preyed on a young girl.

Rainey nodded. "Yeah, I wasn't exactly sober, that's for sure. By the time we got back to his house, there were a ton of Harleys outside. Music was pumping out the windows and people were everywhere. Clearly they were having a party. And you know how much I love a good party."

She slipped her hands out of mine and sat back against the bench. "One thing led to another and suddenly I woke up hungover in Hawk's room."

My hands gripped the wooden bench underneath me, in danger of breaking the whole fuckin' thing. I might be sick.

Rainey laughed, but the sound was empty. "I wasn't the only

one in Hawk's bed. I quickly learned that he had several girl-friends and this wasn't a random party. He was part of a motor-cycle club. A rough one. He was sweet to me for a whole week, making me feel like I was special. He even kicked the other girls out of his room when I said it made me uncomfortable. But things changed quickly. He grew tired of me, and one night when there was another party, he told me if I didn't let him bring the girls back in, he was going to share me with his friends so I understood how things worked around there."

I stood abruptly, pacing the small area under the bridge just to burn off some steam. I was going to fuckin' kill that bastard. I'd hunt his ass down and make his death long and painful for what he'd done to Rainey.

I could feel her watching me, probably wondering if she should continue. "Lawson was there."

"What?" I spun to face her, ready to march into Crazy Beans and beat the shit out of him too.

Rainey held her hand out. "That's why I was talking to him just now. I saw the club's tattoo on his forearm and he finally recognized me. He apologized for not helping me get out." Rainey stood, putting her hand on the center of my chest. "And I did get out, Zeke. I made sure Hawk was nice and drunk, then snuck out before the sun came up. I hitched rides until I got to Colorado and found a job. He never came looking for me and I have him to thank for growing up real freaking fast."

I ran both hands through my hair, pulling at the strands just to distract myself from the anger coursing through my veins. "You shouldn't have had to, Rain. Why didn't you come back to Blueball? I would have taken care of you."

Her gaze dropped to my chest. "I was embarrassed. I'd left here like a bat out of hell. How could I come back just two weeks later with my tail between my legs?"

My arms fell to my side and her hand slid off my chest. I could see how glossy her eyes had gotten again, and even though I was mad at her, mad at Hawk, mad at the world right now, I loved her more than all of that. I could figure out my anger later. Right now, Rainey needed me. I pulled her close and wrapped her in my arms, feeling her body shake as she cried against my chest.

I wasn't sure how much time passed, but eventually I led her back to my truck and we went home, neither of us saying another word. I wasn't sure if Rainey was back in that place, reliving her experience, or if she was embarrassed now that she'd told me what happened. I wasn't speaking because I didn't trust myself to say the right thing, not when I was still reeling from her story.

As we climbed the steps to my front door, I hung back. Rainey pushed the door open and looked over her shoulder. Daisy came barreling out the door and batted her nose against Rainey's hand until she petted her.

"I, uh, have a job to get to. I'll be back as soon as I can and we'll make dinner together." Without waiting for a reply, I spun around and left. I did have some work to do, but all of it could have waited. I just couldn't be around her and not rage about the things that had happened to her. The last thing she needed was me losing my shit twelve years too late and rehashing all of the trauma.

I did eventually go home and make dinner with her, keeping my rage down to a quiet simmer below the surface. My hands ached from chopping wood. The knuckles on my right hand were split. Found out it hurt like a son of a bitch to punch a tree trunk when you were mad. I hadn't come to any conclusions about what to do with the story Rainey had told me, but I knew it wasn't dead and buried. I wasn't sure I'd ever get over it.

But every night I'd kissed Rainey on the forehead and pull her into my chest as we spooned in bed, thanking whatever god watched over me that she hadn't chosen that day to leave me. I didn't make a move to get her out of those hideous flannel pajamas and she didn't make a move either. We talked about all the little things that happened in our day, but we didn't touch the subjects neither of us were prepared to discuss: her thoughts on leaving town and her past that didn't involve me. We danced around both topics, evidenced by a lull in conversation that happened every so often. I didn't know if those lulls would decrease in number as time went on or become so suffocating that this sham marriage would dissolve under the pressure.

I was giving her space to figure out what she wanted to do with her life. I wouldn't be the asshole who influenced her to stay just so I would be happy. Rainey deserved to make decisions on her own now that she was an adult and had the means to do whatever she wanted.

I just hoped she'd eventually choose me.

ainey

THE TRUCK BOUNCED over the bumps and dips of the dry field on the outskirts of Blueball as we looked for a parking space. The barren landscape had been revived with the structures of the carnival the Blueball city council put on every year. The yearly event had been named the Blueball Summer Crawl for as long as I'd known it existed. It was a family affair, despite the reference to a beer crawl, though that happened too. The city council set up a long line of rideshares to make sure everyone got home safe, but unlike when I was in high school and had to sneak the alcohol, I was looking forward to drinking out in the open this time.

Zeke had one hand up on the steering wheel, his thumb tapping out a rhythm to the country song playing softly on the radio. His other hand lay in a tight fist on his thigh, unlike when I'd first arrived when he would have had my hand tangled in his. I sighed quietly, wishing this space he'd put between us for the last week was gone. I'd quit thinking about Hawk and all that had happened there pretty much right after I told Zeke about it. I'd had twelve years to process that messy time in my life and I'd found some peace. Cleary, Zeke had not.

I glanced down at the jean skirt I'd put on for tonight. It was short by even a teen's standard. I'd worn it specifically for getting that flame to burn hot in Zeke's eyes. The one that had been missing for a week now. I wasn't one to sit back and let things happen to me, so I'd decided to take matters into my own hands. Starting tonight.

If I was staying here—and that was definitely still up in the air—then I wanted to take advantage of marital relations, if you catch my drift. I'd had one glorious taste of Zeke's naked body over mine and I craved more. Snuggling my backside up against him every night wasn't cutting it anymore, and based on the erection pressing back, it wasn't enough for Zeke either.

Zeke found a spot and put the truck in park, hopping out and coming around to help me down from his truck. I had to work to keep the mischievous grin off my face as I "stumbled" getting out of the truck and accidentally slid down his body. My cowboy boots hit the ground with a small puff of dirt and I leaned my head way back to smile up at my date.

"What shall we ride first, husband?"

Zeke's jaw tightened and I had an even harder time tamping down the smile. Fair was fair. He'd been calling me wife since the moment we said I do. He didn't answer me, but he did lace his fingers through mine and tugged me toward the entrance. He took care of purchasing the tickets, even when I offered to pay.

"We're on a date, Rain. I'm fuckin' paying," he growled, not caring one bit that my bank account was stuffed to the gills and willing to be spent.

I hugged his arm as we walked through the turnstiles and debated which row of games to walk down. Obviously I'd liked Zeke when I lived here before. We were best friends, after all.

But this time around, I had at least some level of maturity to see that he really was the nicest man I'd ever met. He could growl and pout and be generally disagreeable just like anybody, but underneath all that bluster was a heart of gold. And I really, really liked that.

Maybe even *loved* that.

"They better not let our star pitcher near the milk bottle toss!" A guy with dark hair clapped Zeke on the shoulder, his other arm around a pretty woman who had two kids in tow.

"Diego," Zeke said, shaking the guy's hand. "Meet my wife, Rainey. Rainey, this is Diego and Mandy. They own Grass."

I shook their hands, happy to see Zeke have friends in town. "Nice to meet you. I've been wanting to try your restaurant."

"Maybe you can get this husband of yours to take you out on a date, huh?" Diego teased Zeke.

"Worry about your own date, ass—dude." Zeke barely corrected himself in time, tossing an apologetic smile to Mandy.

She shrugged and pointed her thumb at her husband. "Like they've never heard those words with this guy around."

They walked off, the kids tugging them toward the carnival games for kids. Zeke took my hand again and we walked to the basketball game where Zeke handed over a couple bucks in exchange for miniature-sized basketballs.

"Pitcher, huh? Still doing that?" It occurred to me that there was a lot I didn't know about Zeke in the years I was gone. After my explanation about Hawk, we hadn't talked about anything deeper than what we wanted to make for dinner that night.

Zeke gestured for me to go first. I hit the button and the countdown started. I tossed the first ball and it didn't even hit the rim. Shit. I tried another and got a little closer. Zeke didn't laugh at my attempts, but I wouldn't have blamed him if he did. This was harder than it looked. Then again, I hadn't attended a carnival since I last lived in Blueball.

"I still pitch for the town softball league."

I looked over at him. "Why haven't you taken me to a game?"

He shrugged and handed me another ball, which I shot and almost made in. "Figured I'd get back to it later."

His words hung there between us, the meaning clear. He'd get back to it later...after I left Blueball again. The loud buzzer made me startle and the carnival worker shot me a look that said he wasn't impressed with my one measly point.

"How about we go bust down some milk bottles?" I said with false brightness, wanting to change the subject.

Every part of me wanted to put his fears to rest. To tell him that I was staying, that his constant monitoring of my whereabouts was unnecessary. But I couldn't. I couldn't give him that kind of hope until I was certain about my future. I didn't even know why I was still here. Okay, that wasn't true. I knew why I was still here and his hand was currently on my back and steering me down the dirt aisle until we got to the game I knew he'd ace.

Zeke handed over some cash. He had that little grin on his face that made my toes curl. "Stand back, lil' lady," he said with an exaggerated drawl, pushing me out of his way and warming up his shoulder.

A few people stopped behind me and watched. Zeke tossed the ball up an inch in his hand, testing the weight before winding up and throwing it square into the tower of bottles and toppling them all. The carnival worker rolled his eyes. Zeke threw the next two balls and took down the other two towers of bottles to the applause from the small crowd behind me. He looked down at his feet, shy all of a sudden, and my heart decided to skip a beat and then race. Yep. There was exactly one very handsome reason I was staying in Blueball when I normally would have left already.

And I was pretty sure I was developing feelings that went way beyond friendship.

Zeke handed over a few more dollars and waved me over. "Your turn, wife."

I stepped up to his side, feeling all eyes on me. I used to

crave the attention from anyone I could get it from. Now I just cared that Zeke was looking at me with all the warmth of the summer sun that had set behind the pine trees. I held the first ball in my palm and decided to have some fun.

"How about we make a little wager?"

He scraped his hand over his jaw, the short whiskers making noise against the calluses of his palm. "I'm listening."

"For every bottle I knock over, I get a kiss."

Zeke's body went still, but his eyes said it all. The deep blue ignited. "I'm in."

I threw the first ball and it hit the backdrop with a thump. Not one bottle even rattled. Someone chuckled behind me and I ignored them to focus on the next ball. I wanted a kiss, dammit.

The next one knocked over the top bottle, the one below wobbling, but not falling. I turned to face Zeke, my face upturned and my lips puckered. He huffed a laugh, but obliged, pecking my lips with all the warmth of a politician kissing the bald head of a baby. I narrowed my eyes at his look of innocence.

"Maybe if you knock over two..." he drawled.

With a growl, I let the third ball fly. The ting of the ball hitting bottles sent a thrill through my body. Three bottles tumbled to the ground. I turned around triumphantly to the cheers of the townsfolk who'd stayed to watch. Zeke hooked a hand around my waist and hauled me against him. A wolf whistle cut through the night air. Then he dipped me over his arm in a movie-worthy kiss, his lips warm and eager against mine. He took his time, exploring my mouth and ignoring everything going on around us. By the time he set me upright, I couldn't have stood on my own two legs if I tried.

"One more ball, miss," the carnival worker said, nudging the last ball closer to my hand. I picked it up without looking away from the heated gaze of Zeke. I threw it and it missed by a long shot.

Zeke shook his head. "That's a damn shame. Watch how it's done, Rain." He let me go to throw a few more dollar bills on the counter. He took the balls in hand and stood even further back than you had to and let them fly, one at a time, knocking every single bottle in the booth down onto the dusty ground. The crowd cheered and the carnival worker presented me with a giant stuffed blue ball.

"Seriously?" I said on a laugh, looking at the hideous prize.

The crowd disbursed, but Audrey, Marlo, Paisley, and Keva remained, their men glued to their sides.

"Showoff!" Gannon hollered at Zeke.

"Can we get beer now? We've earned it, haven't we?" Lincoln asked the group.

We looked around at the various prizes clutched in the women's hands. Our men had all shown off for us here at the Summer Crawl. The least we could do was reward them with a cold beer. We all headed for the food vendors, selecting equally unhealthy fried food items and overflowing beer cups, and meeting back at a picnic table. There wasn't room for all of us to sit, so Zeke sat and pulled me onto his lap, feeding me a corn dog so good I let out a groan each time I took a bite. Conversation flowed and we might have been the loudest table with all the teasing and laughing.

At one point, with my belly full and my heart feeling even fuller, I laid my head down on Zeke's shoulder and closed my eyes to take it all in. I was happy. I'd made friends here. Why in the world would I even be considering leaving Blueball again?

Zeke nudged me. "Falling asleep, baby girl?" he whispered.

I kissed his neck before I thought about it. "Nah. Just happy." Then I remembered my goal tonight. To get Zeke and I back on a good path. One that led to intimacy and more nights exploring each other's bodies.

"Want to make me even happier?" I asked coyly.

"Always."

He was such a good man. I lifted my head and looked him right in the eyes. "Take me to our spot."

Zeke didn't even hesitate. He just put his hand on the table, pushed me upward so I stood, and told the group we were leaving. They gave us shit, but I let it wash over me. I was sure they all knew what we were getting ourselves into. I just hoped Zeke was on board with that plan.

We got back in the truck and drove to the park, holding hands as we walked through the dark. The park was deserted, as the whole town was over at the Summer Crawl. We got to our spot, the bench barely visible in the dark shadow under the bridge. Zeke sat first, then tugged me onto his lap like we'd been sitting at dinner. I slid my arms around his neck and kissed him, not waiting one more second for him to make the first move. He responded with a groan, his tongue immediately jumping into action and taking the kiss deeper.

"Zeke?" I gasped, pulling away just enough to speak. He bit lightly into my bottom lip and then we were back to kissing. Without disconnecting, I pulled my leg over his lap and straddled him. My short skirt pushed up indecently high on my thighs and his hands took advantage, squeezing my flesh all the way up to the juncture at the top. My underwear was already soaked, which he'd find out soon if he kept exploring.

"Rain," Zeke groaned into my mouth, his hands stilling before they got to where I needed him most.

I took matters into my own hand, in the back of my mind amazed at how aggressive I was being. I'd never been like this before, but Zeke made me feel safe. I unbuttoned his jeans and slid down the zipper.

"Here?" Zeke said, his voice catching.

"Yes, please," I begged, my hips already rocking against the steel length below me.

"Fuck, Rain," he growled, sliding his arms around me to lift us up enough to shove his jeans down. His erection popped free, and a second later, I had my hands on it. "I don't...shit. Rain, stop."

I stilled, my heart frozen, thinking he was about to say no.

"I don't have a condom on me."

"I'm on birth control." And quite frankly, I didn't want anything between us. Not the silence and careful movements of this last week. Not even a condom.

He studied me in the darkness, only the biggest of details visible. When he nodded, I didn't waste any time. His thumb held my damp underwear to the side. I lifted up using my thighs and notched him at my entrance. I slid downward, one glorious inch at a time until he filled me so completely all I could do was rest my forehead against his shoulder.

"Rain," he muttered, sounding as overcome as I was. We hadn't even started moving yet.

I lifted my head and held on to his shoulders. "Don't hold back." I lifted up and slammed back down, the pleasure of the tight squeeze so good I wanted to keep my eyes shut. I wouldn't though. I wanted to see every expression flick across Zeke's face. I wanted to see his jaw harden and that vein on the side of his temple throb. I wanted to see how his fingers gripped my hips so tightly I'd have bruises tomorrow. And I definitely wanted to remember the sight of him thrusting up into me when I took too long to lift back off of him.

"Oh my God," I chanted, the cool evening breeze hitting my heated skin, but doing nothing to cool things off between us. My shins ached from using the wood bench for leverage, but I pushed away the pain to focus on the intense pleasure of each lift and fall.

When Zeke shifted a hand, his thumb strumming across my clit, there was no keeping quiet. I mewled into the night, the first wave of orgasm taking over as he pistoned wildly up into me. He cursed, the rumble of his voice adding to every sensation bombarding me. I held on for dear life, letting him prolong my orgasm as he caught up. As he spilled into me, I finally laid my head down on his shoulder, the image of his face burned into my memory. Zeke unleashed was the hottest thing I'd ever seen.

Before I was ready, Zeke was pulling my skirt down over my ass, as if he was afraid someone would happen to walk by and see us. I began to giggle, imagining their face if they did. He twitched inside of me and the laughter dried up immediately. He pushed hair away from my heated skin and cupped my face.

"Let's go home, wife."

eke

"FUCK!" I snatched my hand back and shook out the pain immediately pounding in my thumb.

That was what I got for taking my mind off of what I was doing, which was building a gate after I'd finished a long line of fencing earlier this week. Too bad my brain was completely focused on the way Rainey had tipped her head back while I was buried inside of her, her long throat highlighted by the moonlight that crept under the bridge that night. Our spot had never looked so fuckin' good with Rainey moaning while straddling me.

Ten minutes later I dropped the end of a two-by-four on my foot and decided to call it a day before I ended up severely maimed by my own incompetence. Maybe a quick power nap was in order. I cleaned up my worksite and then tossed my tools in the back of my truck. I'd have to come back tomorrow and regroup. I'd also need to get better sleep tonight if I hoped to finish the project.

That thought made me grin while I started the truck and headed home. I'd been up all night with an insatiable bride. All the tension between us over the last week had exploded into a need to devour each other. Repeatedly. I couldn't believe we'd made love outside under the bridge, where anyone could have seen us. Then again in the truck at home. And in our bed every night thereafter. My body was completely satiated and my left hamstring was fuckin' sore, but my head was not at peace.

The thought of her leaving was like a black cloud that descended at random times and ruined my day. It just killed me that we could be this happy together and Rainey was still thinking of leaving. What did I need to do to get her to love me? Was that even the right question? Forcing a woman to love you didn't seem like the best move for lasting happiness, yet that was where my brain went every single time. I'd tried to show her how much I loved her, but it was like throwing pebbles into the ocean. The waves kept coming and the pebbles just sank to the bottom, unnoticed and ineffective.

Mom's ten-year-old SUV was parked in my driveway when I got home. She was sitting in one of the deck chairs out on my porch, just rocking back and forth and staring out at the yard. I knew Rainey wouldn't be here. The girls had invited her to lunch today and Audrey had volunteered to swing by and pick her up. I was always happy to see Mom, but kind of bummed about losing my nap time.

"Hey, Mom," I called as I exited the truck and hit the stairs. I leaned down to give her a kiss on the cheek before sitting in the chair next to her. "This is a lovely surprise."

Mom's mouth pulled into a small smile. "Sure. What man doesn't love his mother coming over unannounced?"

I was just happy to see her smiling. There was a time there when she didn't smile for months. "I'm not most men."

"No, you're not. Which is why I'm here."

That didn't sound good. "Okay..."

Mom pinned me with the look all mothers perfect when they

want the truth out of their spawn. "Gertie told me about Rainey's inheritance. And the stipulations." She let that announcement hang there.

Guilt felt worse than slamming a hammer on my thumb. "You should work for the CIA," I grumbled.

Mom simply lifted an eyebrow.

I sighed. There was no use lying to her further. I respected my mother and she deserved the truth. She'd find out anyway as soon as Rainey got bored and left me again.

"Rainey came back to town to get married so she could inherit." I ran a hand over my face. Fuck, this was hard to admit. I knew she'd be disappointed. "She was going to marry some idiot who didn't deserve her. You know how I feel about Rainey."

Mom reached over and held my hand. "You've always loved that girl. I think from the first moment you saw her."

My lips jerked into a smile, a reflex of thinking back on that moment. I'd met her on our first day of freshman year. I was assigned the locker right below hers. I saw a pretty new girl and dipped my head, crouching down right at her feet to get to my locker, too shy to say anything. She'd looked down at me and quipped something about men falling at her feet. I'd looked up, and with the halogen hallway lights above her, she looked just like an angel. I carried her books, showed her where her first class was, and the rest was best friend history.

"I couldn't let her marry that guy, Mom. I stepped in and married her so she could get her inheritance."

Mom patted my hand. "No, you didn't."

I swung my head to gape at her.

She pursed her lips. "You married her because you saw an opportunity to finally make her yours. You married her because, even after all these years, you still love her."

I felt about two feet tall as Mom gave voice to my inner most feelings and motivations. Was I that obvious? Was I just some lovesick puppy dog, following Rainey around with heart eyes?

"Don't look so surprised, Ezekiel. I know you better than anyone on this green earth now that your father is gone." Mom looked heavenward like she always did when she spoke about Dad. "What I'm worried about is Rainey. I can see the love on her face when she looks at you, but at her core, she's a runner. Always has been. You can't tame that, son. If you want to keep her you need to make sure she never feels powerless."

"I would never—"

"You took away her choice on who to marry, didn't you?"

My mouth dropped open again. "How did you—"

"Wendy and I are friends and she saw what you did outside the courthouse." Mom shrugged, like that explained everything. "Small towns don't lend to secrets."

I sagged back in my chair. "Well, shit."

Mom snickered. "I may be getting old, but I'm still a mom. I have eyes and ears all over this town and don't you forget it, young man."

"Yes, ma'am." The response was automatic.

"But here's what I'm worried about more than anything," Mom said, leaning over the side of the chair and getting into my space. "Love can never work when it's a one-way street, no matter how badly you want it to work. While you make sure you're what Rainey needs, you make sure she gives you what *you* need too. You deserve to be loved like I loved your father. Wholly, completely, forever."

Mom's eyes filled with tears and so did mine. I remembered all the times I'd catch them holding hands, sneaking kisses, or whispering secrets softly between them. Mom and Dad had been relationship goals. And she was right. I wanted what they had. I'd been so focused on being there for Rainey I'd forgotten what I needed.

"I love you, Mom."

Mom stood and cupped my face. She smelled like lemons and home, so familiar I could have been five years old, sitting on her lap, and I wouldn't have felt more comforted than I did in this moment.

"And I love you, son."

She left, even though I offered to make her lunch. She said I looked tired and needed a nap. Moms were never wrong and their intuition was eerie. She'd gotten me thinking though and I had too much nervous energy to nap. Instead, I changed into workout shorts, foregoing a shirt altogether due to the scorching afternoon sun. I went out back with Daisy and chopped more firewood until my sweaty hands started slipping on the axe. Then I dropped and belted out as many pushups as I could without face-planting. Daisy licked my face, thinking we were playing a game, and I tried to push her away in between reps. When my chest was on fire, I hopped up to the lowest branch of the tree to the left of the house and began to belt out pullups.

All the while my brain was spinning. I wasn't sure if Rainey could love me back the way I needed. She hadn't grown up with Daniel and Emily Burns. She hadn't seen their example of true love to know how it played out in real life. She was so independent due to her childhood that maybe she couldn't begin to meld her life with another's. Maybe all this had been for nothing. Maybe I'd done exactly what I feared the second I saw her back in Blueball.

I'd fallen in love with her all over again, this time as an adult, where the stakes were higher. Odds were good she'd leave again, and instead of being brokenhearted like before...I'd be devastated.

CHAPTER TWENTY

Rainey

"So...shorts can be knitted?" I asked carefully.

Marlo had saved a seat for me right next to her at lunch, either a gesture of goodwill, or a means to keep an eye on me, I wasn't sure. What I did know was that she had a pile of yarn on her lap and two knitting needles while she furiously knotted it all together and ignored her actual lunch. We were at Grass since I'd told the girls I'd never been and they said that was a damn shame. They were right. I would marry this steak salad if I wasn't already married.

"Anything can be knitted, Rainette." Marlo didn't look up, her fingers moving so quickly I couldn't figure out how she was getting all that yarn to patch together. Oh yeah, Marlo also insisted on using my full name, like I was in trouble with the principal or something.

"They had this whole thing. Milly knitted a hideous green sweater for Vander as a show of her love for her grandson, so when Marlo fucked things up with Vander, she knitted him apology pants," Paisley told me around a mouthful of mashed potatoes.

Marlo shot Paisley a nasty look, but didn't dispute the facts. Audrey started giggling, placing her iced tea glass down before she choked on the liquid. "Oh my God, the princess dress!"

All the girls cracked up, even Marlo, who also let out a full-body shiver.

"Wait, that was the night you showed up in town, Rainey," Keva said, leaning over the table. "Marlo had just made up with Vander and then you showed up and Zeke was upset and then the boys all got him drunk."

I winced, remembering how Zeke had smelled like the bottom of a beer keg the next morning when we ran into each other. "Why'd they get him drunk?"

Paisley sucked air in between her teeth. "Well, Rainey girl, it's no secret you did a number on Zeke when you left. The boys, in the spirit of bromance, all got drunk with him so he could deal with the shock of seeing you again. Back in town with another man, no less."

All eyes were on me. I could feel their judgement crawling along my skin. And I deserved it. "The boys are good friends?"

All the heads nodded and that made me feel slightly better. Zeke deserved good friends. Better friends than I'd ever been to him. What had I ever done to deserve his level of friendship? In high school I'd been a whirling dervish of energy, flitting from this exciting thing to the next. I hadn't given him more than my free time when it was convenient for me. Since I'd been back, it had been largely the same. Zeke bent over backwards for me and I...well, what did I do for him?

I looked over at Marlo. "So...apology pants. That tactic worked, eh?"

Marlo pointed a knitting needle at me. "Yes. Vander and I do cute things like that for each other, and if you make fun of me, I'll jab this knitting needle in your eye."

Perhaps I should have been offended by the threat, or at least put off by the harsh tone of it, but I was starting to get the feeling that Marlo was just being Marlo. Under that prickly exterior was a warm beating heart. Deep, deep inside. Maybe.

However, an idea had formed and I was humbled enough to ask for what I needed. "I was actually hoping you could teach me to knit."

Marlo dropped her hand and stared at me, her gaze dancing around my face before she smiled. I blinked. I had never seen her smile before. And she was stunningly beautiful.

"No. Absolutely not."

I opened my mouth to beg, but she cut me off.

"You have to find your own way to apologize. Something that means something to Zeke."

"She's right," Keva piped up. "If you're looking to apologize or just do something nice, you have to find what makes Zeke tick. We all know what our men need."

Audrey nodded enthusiastically. "Boston acts all tough, but when I pull out my harmonica, he's on me instantly." She fanned her face and the girls chuckled.

"I start a fight." Paisley got a look on her face that was pure evil. "My cowboy loves nothing more than my smart mouth. The makeup sex is in-fucking-credible."

The girls kept talking but I tuned them out as my brain spun. I wanted to do something for Zeke, but had no idea what. And what did that say about me? I had no freaking clue what my best friend-slash-husband liked? I was a pitiful human being who had no right to be showered with his kindness on a daily basis.

My chair scraped back as I stood suddenly and all heads swiveled in my direction. "Gotta go."

I ran to the door, ignoring Audrey calling out that she'd driven me here. I had my man to get to. I had amends to make. Things to learn about Zeke Burns. Riding high on this newfound friendship with a gang of weird but sweet girls was feeding my brain all kinds of creative ideas. Dreams for the future were manifesting when all I'd seen before was a giant question mark stretching out for years to come. Why *not* stay in Blueball? Why not see what future Zeke and I could have? I wasn't sure what love was, but I felt safe around him. I looked forward to talking to him. I wanted to do nice things for him. I wanted to make future plans with him. Was that love?

I felt called to find out.

His house was only a mile and a half outside of town, but my legs and lungs were burning when I finally made it. He wasn't inside and neither was Daisy, but his truck was parked outside. I opened the back glass slider and nearly stumbled to a stop. Found him.

He was currently hanging from a tree, sweat dripping down from his tanned shoulders to his spine, sliding into the band of his shorts slung low on his hips. His muscles rippled and flexed as he brought his head above the tree branch and then lowered again. Pullups. He was doing pullups. I had to wipe my chin, pretty sure I was drooling. The man was gorgeous, all lean brawn packaged in tan smooth skin.

He dropped to the ground and picked up a tennis ball, making Daisy turn in a frenzied circle, barking her head off. He cocked it back and threw it, the dog tearing off in a mass of fur. He shouted for her and she caught it in midair before landing and racing back to him. He fell to his knees and Daisy barreled right into him, knocking him over in a tussle with Zeke's uninhibited laughter ringing out. He held her snout off of him with a single hand, but that didn't stop Daisy's tongue from venturing out and swiping him across the face to more laughter. I focused on the hand holding the dog. The one with the gold band shining in the afternoon sun.

Zeke Burns was my *husband*. The ring said he was *mine*.

And if that lurch in my chest was anything to go by, I liked my husband.

Very much.

I put two fingers to my mouth and whistled. Both dog and man froze, then rolled to standing. They had weeds and leaf debris clinging to them, and oddly enough, they were smiling like twins. Daisy's smile used more tongue, but honest to God, they looked identical.

"You're home," Zeke said, breaking from the staredown first and walking over. Daisy followed, her tail swishing wildly. I reached down to pet her head, but I kept my gaze on Zeke.

He was even hotter from the front. Why did those lines of muscle over a man's hip turn a woman to absolute mush? I wanted to trace them with my tongue while my fingers found every rivulet of sweat sliding between his bulging muscles.

"I'm home," I agreed, the words taking on a meaning much deeper than the simple way I said them. I was starting to think maybe I *was* home. Blueball. This house. Zeke.

Zeke tilted his head, putting his hands on my hips but keeping distance between us. "Everything go okay at lunch?"

I nodded, but plowed ahead with what I'd been thinking about. Not his muscles. I'd show him how I felt about those later. For now, I wanted to rectify my horrible behavior. I wanted to know what made my husband tick.

"Could this work for real?"

Daisy put her paw on Zeke's leg. He snapped his fingers and she let out a whine before turning and sitting on the top step of the deck.

"We wouldn't still be here if this couldn't work," he answered simply. Again, taking the fall and using the word *we* when what we both know he meant was *you*. *I* wouldn't still be here. Let's face it, I was the only one who'd be running away. Zeke was as solid as the roots of that huge oak tree.

"I'd like to try dating you." There. I said it.

Zeke's mouth tipped up on one side. "You want to date me, wife? Isn't that a little backward?"

He was teasing me, and normally I'd live for that level of teasing, but not today. Today I was serious. Today I came to the conclusion I needed to get my life together and not in the way I first thought when I came to Blueball. My life wasn't made by the zeroes of my bank account and the supposed freedom I thought that would give me. It was made by the people I'd connected with recently. I'd come home for all the wrong reasons, but I could stay for the right ones.

"We got it all jumbled. Best friends to strangers to married. We skipped an important step. So yeah, I'd like to officially date you, Zeke."

The man barely waited for me to get his name out before he barreled into me, tossing me up in the air and against his chest. My arms and legs naturally wrapped around him as he ran into the house, forgetting to close the slider. I pointed to the door, about to say something about mosquitoes getting in, but Zeke leveled a heated glare at me, still rushing through the house.

"I have waited sixteen years to hear you say those words, so pardon me if I'm not going to pause another second and close the fuckin' door."

The smile took over my face in equal portion to the joy spreading through my chest. "Where are you taking me?"

It was obvious, but now that I'd said what I needed to say, the teasing was back.

"Where I should have kept you all day today instead of letting you see your friends," he growled, kicking his bedroom door shut with his foot.

My insides clenched in anticipation. I liked this growly side of Zeke. I also liked his laughter. And the way he could make love to me so slow I thought I was going to die from feeling so much all at once.

"But you're all sweaty!"

Zeke pivoted by the edge of the bed, heading instead for the bathroom where he stepped into the large gray-tiled shower and flipped the water valve. He pushed me down his hips and I quit koala-ing him. I barely got my toes on the floor and he was pulling my tank top over my head and tossing the offending material to the side. My shorts and panties were next, shoved down to my feet and removed with my sandals. When he stood back up, his shorts were also missing. It was the fastest I'd ever been undressed.

Zeke held my gaze, stepping into the stream of water and letting it cascade over his head and down his body. My eyes followed the water until it got to his erection. The one already full and straining and bobbing against his lower belly. He gripped himself and growled at me again.

"Get your ass in here, baby girl."

I looked up, pulling on any acting skills I might have buried deep to look offended. "Sex on the first date?"

His grin was positively untamed. "Be a dirty girl and come on my dick."

He didn't have to demand it twice. I was done teasing, done denying the chemistry we had together. I jumped and Zeke caught me, spinning me around until my back hit cold tile. His mouth was on mine in an instant, stealing every cry and moan as he rubbed his dick against my slick folds but didn't enter me. I could come just from his throaty growls vibrating against my chest. God, I was so close.

"Beg for it," Zeke murmured against my skin, his mouth trailing down my neck and dipping further to flick my nipple with his tongue. Where had this assertive, demanding side of my best friend been all this time? My quick inhale made me realize I freaking loved it.

"Please, Zeke, please." I would beg every day and night if he wanted. I had no room for pride when I'd ripped it all to shreds by leaving this man in the first place.

"Please, what?" he said, grinning as he lifted his head.

That smile. It was everything.

"Please give me that dick and make me come," I said slowly, staring deep into his eyes, hoping he could see how much I trusted him. "I want to be *your* dirty girl."

With another growl, he entered me, all bazillion inches of him pulsing inside my flesh while I thrashed against the wall. His hips pistoned in and out, no finesse, no holding back. Just me and him and the need to be one, even if just for stolen minutes in the shower.

And when I came, it was definitely on his dick and I didn't feel like a dirty girl at all.

I felt like his.

CHAPTER TWENTY-ONE

eke

"Do you want me to knit you something?"

Rainey was tracing her finger across my chest, outlining each of my muscles and making me ticklish. I snatched her hand in mine and brought it to my lips to kiss each digit. My chest rumbled with barely awake laughter.

"Why would I want you to knit me something?"

She shrugged, her breast moving against my ribs and making me feel like waking her up three times last night had somehow not satiated anything. "Marlo is knitting Vander a pair of shorts."

That had me cracking up. Rainey's head bounced on my chest and she swatted at me to calm down. "I've seen him in his knitted apology pants. I don't want anything like that. There's a small hole on the back where she dropped a stitch or two and believe me when I say no one needs to see that much of Vander's ass."

"Maybe I could sew you a shirt?" She lifted her head. "Or design you a logo for your company? I saw you don't have one."

I tilted my head to look at her, wondering where all this was coming from. "I mean, sure. If you want to."

Her eyes lit up. "What's your favorite color? And do you like cartoon-type drawings or the, like, geometrical-type logos?"

"Um, blue and shapes, I guess." I rolled into her and clamped my fingers on her lips. "Enough with the questions, chatterbox. I need breakfast first."

When I let her go, she snapped her teeth at me playfully before disentangling and springing out of bed. I watched her bounce away, enjoying the view of her ass and legs and the way the ends of her hair flitted against her spine. Fuck, she was beautiful.

"What can I make? What's your favorite breakfast?" she asked while scooping my shirt off the ground and pulling it over her head. Fuck me, now she was even hotter, standing there naked under my T-shirt.

"Whatever has protein and keeps me full?" What was with the questions this morning? I didn't necessarily mind it, though it was different.

She opened her mouth, no doubt to play a game of Would You Rather, breakfast edition, but her phone buzzed on the bedside table where she had it plugged in and charging. She scooped it up and made a face.

"What?" There it was again, that black cloud casting shade over an otherwise perfect morning. I was instantly on alert, expecting bad news.

"It's Grandma Gertie. She wants to know if they can throw us a wedding reception or if we're still in our honeymoon phase."

That wasn't bad news. I slid my hand up the back of her bare thigh to squeeze her ass under the hem of the shirt. "Still in our honeymoon phase," I grunted. Rainey smirked and moved out of ass-grabbing range. She bit her lip as she moved her thumbs over the phone screen, which meant she was thinking. Hard. "Wait, has she been asking a lot?" Rainey hadn't said anything about pressure from her grandma.

She put the phone down and edged toward the doorway, not making eye contact. "Uh, yeah. Pretty much every other day."

I swung my legs over the side of the bed and pulled on a pair of workout shorts I'd folded but forgotten to put away. Dread sat like a brick in my empty stomach. "Why don't you want them to?"

She shrugged her shoulders. "I don't know. Seems like a lot of work for an old lady. She just doesn't need to do that." She rapped her knuckles against the doorframe. "Last chance to choose: omelette or french toast?"

"Both," I answered, no longer feeling happy and carefree like I had when I woke up this morning. Rainey may have asked to date me, but her mind was far from made up about leaving. If she already knew she wanted to stay, she would have let her grandma throw us a reception. The excuse about Gertie being old was lame and we both knew it. That woman could dance circles around us both. She went to the gym every single day and played pickleball in the afternoons. The truth was, if Rainey said yes to the party, she'd be publicly locking herself into staying.

"Both it is!" Rainey called, already heading down the hallway.

"Fuck," I muttered to the walls. I thought last night was a turning point in our relationship, but we were still where we'd always been: in limbo.

Breakfast was fantastic, even though I had to dodge more than twenty random questions about my likes and dislikes. It was like Rainey got ahold of some book promising one hundred perfect questions to ask on a first date. When I'd agreed to date her yesterday, I didn't think I was signing up for an interrogation.

Frustrated, I left after I helped clean up the kitchen, using work as an excuse. It was true, I did have a job to get to, but it could have waited if I wanted. I was on edge, happy on the surface but just waiting for the other shoe to drop.

My truck and I wound through the town until I came out the other side. The town cemetery looked both somber and achingly beautiful with the morning sunlight filtering through the tall trees. I'd spent quite a bit of time there after my father passed away and I always appreciated how well Marlo and her family kept the sacred space.

Vander had bought the old Skinner House next door to the cemetery. I'd been doing quite a few projects for him since he moved here. We were in the process of converting the rambling house into a senior center, complete with owner's quarters in the back. He and Marlo already had five seniors staying with them and had capacity for three more if I could get the last few rooms finished. Today, he wanted to talk to me about the possibility of turning one of the four garage bays into an air-conditioned therapy room for his seniors. My reply was that everything was possible with enough money, but for my friend, I would try everything I could to keep the costs down. I knew he was a millionaire from selling his prior company, but Blueballers didn't gouge each other.

The doorbell chimes pealed out inside the house as I waited on the huge stone patio out front. The chair lift up the stairs to the front door had streamers tied to the back of it, either an addition by Gertie or Milly. Or possibly both. With those ladies, anything ridiculous was possible. Marlo opened the door and waved me in, her eyes narrowing on my bedhead. In my haste to get out of the house, I forgot to tame the hair that Rainey had gripped in her fists over and over last night.

"You look like you wrestled all night long instead of slept. Should I text Rainey and make sure she's walking okay this morning?" she asked dryly.

I shot her a look of death and destruction, but given she was the queen of both those lands, she was unaffected. "Where's the garage you want me to look at?"

Marlo huffed. "Oh, it's like that, huh? Okay, I'll play along." She put her hands to her mouth and shouted, "Vander? Zeke's here!"

Instead of summoning Vander, the elderly among them burst

out of the kitchen like they'd been eavesdropping. Gertie approached first, giving me a hug and foisting me on Milly, who also insisted on a hug. Jerry, the surly senior who'd been here right from the start of the senior center, just gave me a head nod. Behind him were two men I hadn't met yet, but they looked vaguely familiar. Probably went to church with Wendy and my mother.

"Buzz and Arthur," Jerry said, then waved a hand at me. "Meet Zeke."

The two men eyed me with interest, elbowing each other over and over, which was weird, but then again, a houseful of seniors was weird in and of itself. I would have expected better behavior from a kindergarten class while their teacher left the classroom to go to the bathroom.

"Zeke!" Vander called from behind me.

I turned to greet him and groaned. "Not the fuckin' apology pants." Marlo smacked the back of my head and I winced. "I mean, they're perfect for a summer day. Got vents and all."

Vander frowned, clearly not understanding the problem with the dropped stitches in the back. Marlo sounded like she swallowed a laugh so at least she knew what I was referring to. The woman probably dropped those stitches on purpose. Vander pulled me into the garage and we discussed all the changes that would need to be made, permits to pull, and problem areas. Once we figured everything out in terms of the layout, I told him I could write up an estimate tonight and email it over.

"Only if you want. You know I'm going to go with you no matter what number you put on that estimate." Vander folded his arms across his chest and leaned back against the rear garage wall. "The work you've done in the bedrooms is top notch."

"Thanks, man. I don't do anything half-ass."

Vander went to say something else, but was cut off by a shriek from a real live banshee inside the house. "Shit." He burst into action, flying back into the house with me hot on his heels.

The scene we found in the front parlor that had become an activity room for the seniors was horrifying.

Jerry was standing on top of a chair with his face red and blotchy while Buzz and Arthur cheered him on. Milly was shouting at him to get down before he broke his short stubby neck. Gertie held up three playing cards and attempted to twerk. Or maybe she was tying her shoe. I wasn't quite sure and I didn't intend to look any longer to find out.

"Hey!" Vander got Jerry down. Marlo ran in and helped Gertie back in her chair. "What is going on here?"

"She cheated!" Jerry shouted, pointing at Gertie, who squawked like she'd been accused of murder.

Milly lifted her nose in the air and waited for the riffraff to quit yelling. "Gertie usually does cheat, but she didn't this time and Jerry can't stand that he's losing."

"He's losing our other bet too," Buzz chided. Arthur cracked up. Jerry's face shifted into something more purple than red.

"What bet? Guys, you know we made a house rule. No betting." Marlo folded her arms across her chest, properly chastising them with her scary frown. "I know where all of you are going to be buried one day and I can make sure all the stray cats piss on your graves."

Arthur dropped the grin immediately, his owl eyes behind coke-bottle glasses looking hurt. "Damn, Marlo, it was just a harmless bet about when Gertie's granddaughter would ditch Blueball again."

"Shh!" Jerry shot his friend a wide-eyed look and then swung his gaze to me.

"What?" Arthur asked, clearly puzzled what had the head senior crony upset.

"Are you kidding me?" Gertie snapped, throwing her cards down on the table.

I was both shocked and humiliated. The seniors of Blueball were betting on when my marriage would implode. They didn't even know it was a marriage of convenience and they *still* thought Rainey would run right out of this town and leave me behind.

Marlo put one hand on Gertie's shoulder and her other on my forearm. "How about you all go back to your rooms? And if you don't drop that bet, I'll kick your asses right out of Skinner House."

"And I'll make sure no other senior homes will take you in either," Vander threatened, clearly angry on my behalf.

The three men scraped back their chairs, but I'd heard too much to stay silent like I normally would. Everyone thought they could push around the quiet guys. Rainey had rolled right over me in high school and apparently thought she could do it still. My mother was right. I had to start standing up for myself and demanding the treatment I deserved.

I lifted my hand and pointed to the three men, pinning them with a look I hoped they wouldn't forget anytime soon. "You're all assholes. You know that, right? I've lived in Blueball my whole life. My dad before me dedicated his entire career to working on your houses. You go to church with my mother, for fuck's sake. And you have the audacity to sit here and place bets on my marriage imploding?" Buzz and Arthur had some semblance of manners as they dropped my gaze to study their white sneakers. "Blueballers don't do that to each other."

Marlo reached for me with both hands now, but I backed up. If I stayed any longer, I might have ended up in a fistfight with some old guys and that wouldn't be what a Blueballer should do either.

"I gotta go." And without another word, I stormed out of the house. I was almost in my truck when Gertie came flying down the front steps far faster than someone her age should. She paused at my door and caught her breath while I tried to tamp down the anger still burning in my chest.

"I'm proud of you, Zeke," she finally said. "I've never seen you act like a honey badger, and I'm just so damn proud you're sticking up for yourself."

This woman had seen me at my lowest points in life, both when Rainey left and when my father died. She'd only had kind words and encouragement for me, almost like a second mother.

I grabbed her hand and held it. "Gertie, you may not be happy with me soon if I keep going down this 'sticking up for myself' path."

She studied my face, understanding dawning. Her eyes went shiny, but she nodded. "You do what you have to do. If Rainey leaves again, that's on her." She let go of my hand to pat my cheek. "I like this version of you, and if she knows what's good for her, she will too."

CHAPTER TWENTY-TWO

Rainey

DAISY HEARD ZEKE FIRST, turning away from my feet where she'd been sitting patiently, waiting for food to drop. The door opened and the sound of his heavy work boots on the wood floors made me smile down at the stove where I was working on my second attempt at lunch. The first attempt was burned to a crisp and at the bottom of the trash can.

"Hey! I made those tuna oatmeal patty things you used to love," I called over my shoulder as he stalked by the kitchen. He'd made them almost daily when we were teens in his quest to put on muscle. Based on his size now, they worked. He paused, turning toward me, but not meeting my gaze.

"Thanks." He spun and thumped away.

My smile fading, I turned off the burner, slid the patties onto a plate, and trailed behind him as he flopped down on the couch in the living room. Setting the plate on the coffee table, I had a seat on the couch with him, leaving space between us. Zeke was not only not good at hiding his emotions, he usually didn't even bother to try. It might have been sunny outside, but thunder-clouds were rolling across his face.

"What's wrong?" I asked quietly, already knowing I'd have to wait him out. He was never one to jump right into sharing his feelings. It usually took countless questions and patient cajoling for him to divulge what was going on.

Zeke leaned forward, his elbows on his knees, his hands rubbing over his face. "I'm just in a bad mood."

"You don't say," I muttered under my breath.

Zeke's head came up and he shot me a dark look. I tried to tease him a bit, hoping to pull him out of whatever mood he'd contracted since climbing out of bed this morning.

"Maybe it's just low blood sugar. Eat some lunch and I bet you'll feel better. These patties are full of protein and so low fat it's disgusting. Like actually disgusting."

Zeke spun the plate around on the table. "Thanks for lunch. I really appreciate it, but I think I just need to be alone for a bit. Get my thoughts together."

"Oh!" I shot to my feet, taken aback. Never in the history of our friendship had Zeke asked to be alone. And I'd seen him in plenty of dark moods. "Sure. Yeah. Um, I was meaning to see Grandma Gertie anyway. Do you mind if I take your truck?"

Zeke was staring at his plate, as if wishing me gone when all I wanted was to run my fingers through his thick hair. Maybe yank his face up to me and kiss away whatever was bothering him. I wanted that little smirk back, the one that said he was trying not to smile at my antics but found me too adorable to wipe the smile completely.

But this was his house and he'd just asked me to leave. To give him space. The poor man had had zero space since I showed up in town. Maybe things had moved too quickly between us. I mean, obviously they did. I had the ring on my finger to prove it, but I thought last night had been a turning point. A promise to try a real relationship. Day one and he was already asking for space?

"Okay, I'll shoot you a text so you know when I'm on my way." I ended that sentence awkwardly. Before I could finish with "home." On my way *home*.

Zeke lifted his gaze long enough to give me a stern nod and then it was back to focusing on the lunch I'd made him, like that tiny plate held all the answers to whatever was troubling him. I wanted to say more, anything to quell this jumpy ache in my belly, but I shut my mouth and headed out the door instead, giving him what he said he needed.

The drive over to the old Skinner House was a silent one. I didn't even bother with music. I was too busy thinking about Zeke and his dark mood and our history and if loving him was possible. Every building I passed to get through town held a memory from high school and right smack-dab in the middle of every single memory was Zeke. I always thought the way my gut turned to liquid hot lava when I remembered each of those moments when I was far away from him was simply nostalgia.

Or was that love? Did love include the excitement I felt this morning working on something that I thought might help his business? Or making him lunch and anticipating seeing his face light up? Or dancing hot and sweaty out in the yard and not caring that all our friends could see us? Or telling him every detail about my life because nothing felt as big and scary when Zeke was holding my hand?

I pulled into the long driveway of Skinner House, head swiveling at the mature trees and then gawking at the sprawling mansion. I shut off the engine and sat there for a moment. I'd never told anyone I loved them. Not once. Well, maybe when I was a little child, but my father had surely not said it back, which taught me it wasn't something worth saying. But it *was* worth saying and I wanted to say it to Zeke. But only if I actually meant it, and I was no more ready to say I love you as I was to say I was for sure staying in town.

Milly answered the door, her face lighting up when she saw me. I was pulled into a hug and then hustled inside, Milly's cane flying around everywhere instead of down on the ground helping her walk. "Oh, Gertie will be so happy you're here!"

I felt guilty for not coming sooner. I'd been busy with that inheritance and everything changing with Zeke, but as Milly rapped on Grandma's door and she answered with even more enthusiasm than Milly, I was glad I was there now.

"Come in, come in." Grandma slid her arm through mine and tugged me into her spacious room. There was a sitting area tucked under a wide window and that was where we sat, Grandma holding my hand between her papery-thin ones and asking me all kinds of questions. I filled her in on all my travels since I'd left Blueball. Sure, we'd talk once a year when I was gone, but the conversation had been lined with conversational bombs we were both trying to tiptoe around, which meant we didn't share much that was personal.

"Enough about me, Grandma." I squeezed her hand when she tried to ask me yet another question. "Tell me what you've been up to."

"Oh, just this and that. Dealing with these old bats." She fluttered her hand in the direction of the door. I laughed, but my gaze caught on a collection of orange bottles on her bedside table.

"You seem to be in good health."

Grandma nodded. "Oh yes, fit as can be. I hit the gym every morning and I've taken up the pickleball."

I grinned. "The pickleball, huh?" I squeezed her hand again. "Then why do you have five medications over there?" I tipped my head toward the table.

Grandma sucked on her teeth. "You weren't supposed to see those." I lifted an eyebrow and she rushed to explain. "It's not a big deal. I had a minor stroke and those are just making sure it doesn't happen again."

"A stroke? Grandma!" I stood up, pacing in front of the love seat. "When did this happen? Why didn't you call me?"

Grandma swiped her thin arm through the air. "Pshh. It wasn't a big deal."

"A stroke is a big deal!" I felt like a bird, swinging my arms about and squawking instead of speaking in a normal voice. "When? What did the doctors say?"

Grandma sat back and patted the seat next to her. Reluctantly I sat, but I stared at her expectantly. She was the only family I had left and suddenly it occurred to me that she was old. Really old. And fallible. And definitely old enough to die right in front of me, leaving me with no one. Most importantly, I'd never thanked her for taking me in and raising me when my father died. I'd been a hellion to raise and she'd done it without complaint. Certainly, the least I could do was say thank you.

"It was about eleven years ago. Old news."

My jaw dropped. "Eleven years ago? Gram, why didn't you tell me?"

Gertie scoffed. "What good would that do? You would have felt obligated to come home and you were very clear you didn't want to stay in Blueball."

I felt my heart break right there on the love seat at the retirement home. Grandma had a stroke soon after I left and hadn't wanted to bother me by calling. For all I knew, the stress of me leaving on the back of a Harley had been what pushed her over the edge medically.

"And I didn't tell you later because of that face right there." Grandma patted my cheeks. "Quit whatever it is you're thinking. I'm fine. I'm better than fine. That scare got me into physical therapy and then the gym and even the pickleball courts. I'm fitter than when I was forty."

A tear slid down my cheek and Grandma shushed me, pulling me into her arms and letting me lay my head on her bony shoulder. "I'm fine, free bird." That made me cry even more. She was the one who had a stroke and she was comforting *me*?

She let me cry until all the tears had dried up. When I lifted my head, she gave me that little smile of hers. "Feel better?"

I shook my head, wiping my face. "Not really. I still feel like I failed you. Failed Zeke. Hurt you both." I shook my head again when she tried to interrupt with some nonsense about my selfishness being perfectly fine. It wasn't fine. "I did hurt you both. And I'm sorry. So incredibly sorry. I'll make it up to you, I promise. Even if I leave Blueball, I won't let the distance come between us this time."

"Oh, child. I only want to see you happy. That's all I want. Have you been happy?"

My gaze skittered away. That was a loaded question. I'd made it through life, but was I happy like I thought I'd be once I escaped Blueball? Pretty sure what I had with Danny wasn't what one would consider happiness. More like a reluctant settling on a life that was mediocre at best.

Grandma saved me from giving a firm answer out loud. "Would you get the box out from under my bed, Rainey? I have some photos from when you were little I think you should have."

I welcomed the change in subject, getting on my hands and knees to retrieve the box and shove it across the carpet to where she sat. It was covered in dust, but once we got it open, we were too busy oohing and aahing over the pictures to care. Grandma had quite the stack of photos for me to take home when I found one that made me pause. It was a photo that Grandma had taken of Zeke and me all dressed for our graduation. Zeke's parents were with us in the picture, their wide smiles full of pride. The next photograph had been just Zeke and me, but his father was off to the side, his gaze firmly fixed on Zeke, a proud smile for his son even from the wings. The love I saw on his face made my eyes burn.

"Grandma? Can I take this one too?"

"Of course, honey. Take whatever you want. These will all be yours someday anyway."

I shook my head. "Nope. You're going to live forever."

Grandma pinned me with a watery stare. "I wish I could, but I believe love lasts forever, so that's what I want you to focus on.

No matter where you go or whether I'm earthside, my love for you continues."

I heaved a big breath in and out, scrambled to my knees, and threw my arms around her frail body. "I love you too, Grandma."

It felt good to finally say it. It felt right. I loved this woman and not just because she said it first. I loved her for taking me in, offering me forgiveness even when I didn't deserve it, and for showing me what unconditional love looked like. I basically abandoned her twelve years ago and she had kept right on loving me, doing what was best for me, even when she was suffering.

When I pulled away, we were both crying. The good kind of crying. The kind that heals emotional wounds.

"How about we do this once a week?" I asked, then tilted my head. "Maybe without all the crying."

Grandma patted my cheeks. "It's a date."

I helped clean up the pictures and shove the box back under the bed. When I stood, Grandma was studying me. I dusted off my hands and faced her scrutiny instead of leaving like I immediately wanted to. Running away had gotten me into too much trouble to continue it.

"What?"

"Decide quickly, Rainette," Grandma said quietly.

I opened my mouth to dispute the idea of me leaving, but she cut me off.

"I know the marriage wasn't for the usual reasons, so save your argument. Decide about Zeke sooner rather than later. That boy doesn't deserve more heartbreak. The longer you stay, the more he'll fall in love with you. Just don't stay because you feel obligated. That's not the kind of love Zeke or you deserve. Stay because you can't imagine living your life without him."

Her words echoed through my mind the entire drive home.

CHAPTER TWENTY-THREE

eke

"I got you something."

I had good intentions of sitting Rainey down when she got back from Gertie's and discussing every single thing between us that had been bothering me. All my cards on the table. Not one word left unsaid this time. I was also prepared as best as I could be to see the backside of her as she ran right out of here and didn't look back.

Instead, I took the item she handed me, something hard and pointy wrapped in plain brown paper. She looked so eager and hopeful, I couldn't point out that buying me things or learning my favorite color or making me breakfast was not what I wanted from her. I wanted her love, her loyalty, her fuckin' pinky promise she would never leave me again. Realizing that maybe she could never say those things, I ripped the paper off and plopped back down on the couch where I'd been when she walked in.

It was a picture of me and Rainey. And my dad.

I felt the couch move as Rainey sat next to me, snuggling into my side to gaze at the old picture in a plain wooden frame. I'd never seen the picture before, probably because the moment frozen in time was our high school graduation and Rainey had left that night.

"I saw this at Grandma's and I had to frame it for you. Look at the way he looks at you." She sniffled and I realized she was crying. Looking down at her, she swiped her hands across her cheeks, but her eyes kept welling up. "I'm sorry I wasn't here. I didn't get to say goodbye to him. Or be here for you. But I knew you'd want to remember how he looked at you."

"Rain," I whispered, placing the frame at my feet and pushing the hair away from her cheeks to cup her face. I kissed her nose and then each eyelid, breathing her in and wondering how I could love someone so much when they also hurt me more than anyone ever had. "Come here."

Our mouths crashed together and clothes found their way to the floor. We came together in a bumbling mash of whispers and gasps and hands stroking every square inch of skin. I was hopelessly in love with her, a refrain that played in the background the entire time I thrust into her. She seemed to say it back in the way her eyes stayed on mine and her hands clutched me tighter to her. Or perhaps a better bet would be that I was imagining things again. We came at the same time and I had to bite back the words that wanted to slip from my lips.

Not tonight.

Maybe tomorrow I'd work up the courage to say what needed to be said. To watch her walk away.

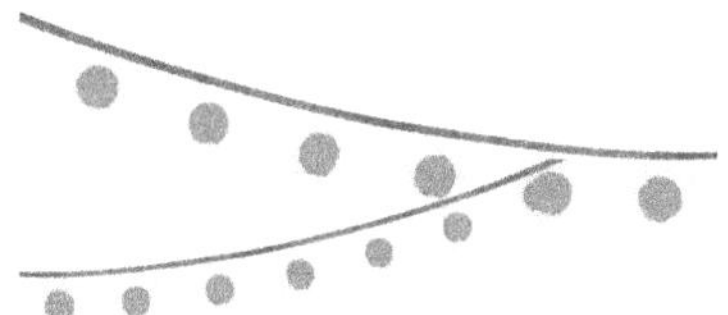

The following week sprawled out on repeat. I spent every hour the sun was in the sky at Glamper's Paradise, helping Gannon build a wood sauna structure that should belong on the cover of a magazine for luxury vacations. When the sunset meant we couldn't see any longer, we called it a day and I went home to Rainey. She made me a late dinner even when I insisted I could put together a simple sandwich. Then we tumbled into the shower or into bed, wrapped up in each other.

And each morning, I would slip out of bed before dawn and head to the jobsite, avoiding the conversation I knew we needed to have. I tricked myself into thinking that this could work. We could live together, fuck together, and even if we never exchanged those three little words, all of the rest would be good enough for me.

"If we don't finish this thing before noon, Paisley might kill me," Gannon said by way of greeting on the sixth day in a row we'd been working on the sauna.

I looked up from the section of deck I was painting with yet another coat of stain. "She in a hurry to get in the sauna?"

Gannon grunted. "No, she's in a hurry for me to have enough free time to swing by her work at noon. She's taken a desk job again and she gets restless. If you know what I mean."

By the sly grin on his face as he picked up a paintbrush, I

knew exactly what he meant. His and Paisley's relationship was something of a role model for me. I gave him shit for being much older than me, but what he had here with his business and what he had with Paisley and their kiddos looked like paradise. They fought like dogs sometimes but then one of them would get a gleam in their eye, and the next thing you knew, the temperature around us rose ten degrees and even a nun would have been feeling horny in their heavy presence.

"You avoiding Rainey already? Aren't you still considered newlyweds?" he asked, his back to me as he painted another section of the exterior of the sauna.

I sighed, too frustrated and beat down with opposing thoughts to avoid his question. "Yeah, I'm avoiding her. Just during the daytime."

Gannon snorted. "I feel you there. I do that sometimes when Paisley's mad at me. I come home when I know she's had time to cool off and we can get right to the makeup-sex part of our argument. It's the key to a successful marriage."

I wished it were that easy. "We're not fighting. Exactly."

Gannon whistled. "That's worse. What's going on?"

My paintbrush stilled, and before I knew what was happening, we were sitting in our boxers inside the sauna, giving the giant machine a test run as I spilled my guts to a genuine friend. He listened, offering short commentary here or there but mostly he just let me vent while we both started to sweat.

"I feel confident on the job, so I rush to get here. Everything at home with Rainey is too jumbled. I feel incompetent there. I guess I'm wavering back and forth between letting things play out as they are with Rainey running right over me again or confronting her for an answer I'm not sure she can give and watching her walk away again."

"That's a fucked-up conundrum, dude," Gannon said finally, leaning back against the molded bench we'd made out of expensive cedar planks earlier in the week.

I wiped the sweat from my forehead, then realized even my forearm was sweating profusely. "Tell me about it."

"Can you live forever with the situation the way it is? You know, with your balls in a Rainey-sized vise?"

I shoved him with my elbow, but slid right off due to all the sweat. "Shut the fuck up."

He waved his hands in the air. "I'm kidding. Kind of. I mean, only you can answer for yourself, but I don't see you settling for a half-ass relationship. You're the type to stick up for what's right. Didn't the girls say you punched a guy junior year who made some lewd remark about Rainey? That's a guy who cares about right and wrong."

My skull made a loud clunk as I tipped my head back against the sauna wall. "Fuck."

Gannon let out a sigh to the ceiling. "Yep. Pretty much."

We didn't end up finishing the sauna by noon, but I did get home just before sunset that day, only to find Rainey missing. Daisy danced around me, wanting my attention, but my gaze was drilled to one spot. There was a letter on the kitchenette table that made my heart stop. For a few awful seconds, I thought Rainey left a note for me and that she was gone. Then I saw the ripped envelope next to the letter and realized it was addressed to her. I scanned the note shamelessly, figuring if she didn't want me to read it, she shouldn't have left it out in the open.

What I read made my heart sink even as the panic receded. It looked like some diner in Colorado had attached her last paycheck, along with a letter on official letterhead. It was from one of her past employers, informing her they'd fired her manager and wanted to rehire her to take his position. Putting the letter back down the way I found it, I called her name. Daisy jumped around in a circle instead of running to find Rainey which told me she was truly not here.

I ran to my bedroom anyway, suddenly needing to see her clothes next to mine in the closet. They were there, hung messily, all pinks and baby blues and flowers next to my boring T-shirts. I sank onto our bed and put my head in my hands.

Gannon was right. I had to do what was right. I couldn't keep living this way, expecting her to leave anytime I turned my back. I told myself that if she told me about the job offer, I'd ask her about her long-term intentions. We'd get it all out in the open. And if she didn't tell me, then I had my answer then too. If she hid it from me, we were definitely done.

"Zeke! What are you doing home so early?" I heard her call from the front of the house. Daisy took off running. I followed at a much slower pace, coming around the corner to see Rainey's face buried in Daisy's neck as the two of them hugged. It was a knife to the chest, seeing my dog love Rainey too. I wasn't the only one who'd miss her when she was gone.

"Got done early and figured we could make dinner together."

Rainey stood and walked over to fling her arms around my neck, a broad smile on her face. "Sounds perfect! I bought every-thing to make enchiladas. Can you grate the cheese?"

We moved about the kitchen making dinner, easily flowing around each other and the conversation mostly one-sided like usual as Rainey regaled me with something that had happened that day. Somehow, the job offer from her old employer hadn't ranked high enough on the list of what had happened that day for her to mention it to me. When we plated our food and Daisy had been fed, I moved to the table.

"Let's eat on the couches!" Rainey suggested, already moving in that direction.

I gave the letter on the table one last look before joining her. We ate, she chatted some more and then snuggled up to my chest while we watched a mindless movie. She fell asleep on my shoulder, her fine blonde hair spreading across my chest. I watched her sleep, memorizing every soft curve of her face, the lift of her chest as she breathed, and the way her fingers twitched as she dreamed.

At some point late in the evening, I picked her up gently and took her to bed, sliding in next to her and letting her snuggle up to me again in her sleep. I let her take comfort in my arms one last time.

Because tomorrow it would all change.

Tomorrow I'd do the thing I had to do.

Tomorrow I'd let my free bird go.

CHAPTER TWENTY-FOUR

ainey

ZEKE WAS GONE by the time I woke up, which wasn't very different from every other morning lately. The man was dedicated to his job, that was for sure. What I couldn't help feeling though was that something was off. Zeke still said all the right things, but that spark in his eye when he looked at me was gone. Had been for over a week now. I couldn't help but feel like that was a failure on my part somehow. Maybe he was getting sick of me. Maybe, just like my father, he realized that taking care of me was simply too much effort.

It was that thought that had me up and dressed around seven and latching Daisy's leash to her collar. We were headed into Blueball to see Lawson. The air-conditioning blast when I opened the glass door of the coffee shop was welcome by the time we made it downtown. Daisy was panting, a situation Lawson quickly noticed. He came around the counter with a bowl of water and set it on the floor for Daisy right by an empty table. The furry thing sank to the cool floor and lapped it up, spilling it everywhere.

"I'll clean that up, promise."

Lawson chuckled. "No worries. What can I get you?"

I straightened my shoulders. "A job, if you still have the position open."

Lawson smiled and wiped his hands on the towel thrown over his shoulder. "You want to work here?"

"Well, I've been working in restaurants since I graduated. Pretty sure a coffee shop isn't too different. I'm a hard worker, so you won't have to wrack your brain for a nice way to fire me."

Lawson laughed and it almost sounded rusty. "I don't wrestle with my conscience when it comes to firing people, Rainey. If they work hard, I pay a more-than-fair wage. If they don't want to work, I show them the door. Easy as that."

"Sounds good to me."

He gestured me over to the counter when a customer came in. I put Daisy's leash on one of the chairs ringing the table and told her to stay. She raised her eyebrows at me as if to say *you think I'm getting up off this cool floor already, lady?*

I waited for Lawson to take the customer's order and spin around to make it on the gleaming machine that let out steam and screeches and grinding noises. He slid the cup across the counter to the customer and turned his attention back to me.

"Come on back here and shadow me for half an hour. If you like it, I'll have you fill out the paperwork on the spot." He shot me a grin. "And pay you for the half hour since I'm a good boss."

The half hour passed in the blink of an eye and I was even more sure I wanted to work there. The bakery chef in the back was a nice middle-aged woman who instantly made me feel welcome. Lawson worked hard, doing absolutely everything needed out front. He told me I'd be mostly working the register and cleaning tables. He'd make the drinks until I felt comfortable doing that too. By the time he tapped his watch and lifted an eyebrow at me, I was all in.

"Let's do it!"

He looked as excited as me when he handed over the employment papers to fill out. "Can I ask you something before you're an employee and technically I shouldn't be asking this?" When I nodded wearily, he continued. "Why do you want to work here? And is your husband okay with you working for me?"

Daisy let out a whine, and because she'd been such a good girl while I shadowed Lawson, I patted my thigh and she came bounding over. Lawson reached for a baked dog treat they sold here. Daisy gobbled it up and gave the huge man heart eyes I didn't think Zeke would appreciate.

"Zeke doesn't know I'm applying," I admitted. "I wanted to surprise him."

Lawson folded his massive tattooed arms over his chest. "Should I watch my back in the parking lot? He didn't look too pleased we were chatting the other day."

"No! He was mad at me that day, you just happened to be in the fallout zone," I said sheepishly. "I want to get a job and show Zeke that I can be an equal partner. I've always relied on him, even in high school. Too much actually. I want him to know that I'm making an effort to build a life with him here in Blueball and that I can stand on my own two feet."

Lawson nodded, as if that was a good enough answer for him. "I'm happy for you, Rainey. I don't know of too many people mixed up in what we were who ended up with a happily ever after."

I wanted to ask him if he had found his happiness, but he inhaled and turned, back to all business. "Bring those back as soon as you can. Anytime you want to start is good for me."

Waving the papers in the air, I picked up Daisy's leash and headed for the door. "I'll be back tomorrow and we can discuss a schedule to start right away."

The walk home felt short. My sandals barely touched the ground, such was my excitement over having a job. And a plan. I hadn't realized how much not making a firm decision about staying in Blueball had been weighing me down. This felt right. Felt good. Felt like the start of the rest of my life.

Because I'd been asking questions recently, I knew that Zeke's favorite food was gourmet pizza and I had all the ingredients at home to make one from scratch. There was even a bottle of champagne in the back of the refrigerator I'd been saving. Tonight seemed like the perfect night to pop it open and celebrate my new life here with Zeke. The wedding had started out as a mere convenience, but it had turned into the best thing that ever happened to me.

I unclipped Daisy's leash once we turned onto the road that led to Zeke's house. She bounded ahead and then dashed back to my side, tongue hanging out the side of her mouth as she ran in circles around me. I thought that might be dog language for *slow poke*.

"Okay, okay, I'll hurry!" I started running and she barked, chasing after me. We were both breathless as we stumbled into the house. "I won!"

I could have sworn Daisy rolled her eyes at me before she buried her snout in the water bowl. Grabbing a water bottle out of the refrigerator, I guzzled it before dropping into a chair by the kitchenette table. A piece of white paper caught my attention. It had black chicken scratch writing on it. I knew right away it was Zeke's handwriting. In high school, I'd pass him a note that had pink lettering covering the entire front side of the paper and he'd send it back with one- or two-word answers on the back that were almost impossible to decipher. Doctors had better handwriting than Zeke. When I gave him crap for it, he simply shrugged and said he preferred to say what needed to be communicated. Considering he didn't talk much either, I thought he was full of shit.

This note wasn't much better than the ones he sent me in high school. It simply said he was spending the evening with the boys and they'd probably be drinking, so he planned to spend the night at Glamper's Paradise. And then he said he'd see me tomorrow.

My heart sank. All that excitement I wanted to share with him disappeared. The worry that something was extremely wrong between us was back. I knew it took a lot to get Zeke to talk about what was bothering him, and at this point, I could only assume he was avoiding me. But nothing was going to be fixed unless we got a chance to talk it out.

I put the note down, realizing the letter from my former employer was underneath. I'd meant to throw it away earlier but had forgotten about it. Folding the final paystub into my wallet, I threw the job offer letter in the trash can. I paced the kitchen, wondering what to do. Previously, I would have shrugged it off and moved on, but I wasn't that naive girl anymore with my head in the clouds. I wanted to face my problems head-on now. Kind of hard to do when your husband wouldn't freaking come home.

Instead of pizza from scratch, I made a peanut butter and jelly sandwich and ate it on the couch while watching *The Bachelor*. Daisy had jumped on the couch with me, even though she wasn't supposed to be up on the furniture. I stroked her soft head and admitted to myself that I was lonely.

I missed Zeke. I missed his grunted answers, his lopsided grin, the way he'd shorten my name to Rain. The look in his eyes when he trained them on me, like I was his whole world and all his focus was reserved for me. The way his rough hands skimmed so carefully across my skin when he made love to me at night. Why had I ever taken all of that for granted? Why had I walked away from the most perfect human I'd ever encountered?

Picking up my phone, I called Grandma. This was also a change for me. The new and improved Rainey reached out to her loved ones when she needed advice or simply a sounding board.

"Rainette?" Grandma said, her voice almost drowned out by hoots and hollers in the background.

"Grandma? What's going on?" I was eating dinner alone in

front of the television while my grandmother was whooping it up at a party. My, my, how the tables had turned.

I heard a door slam and then the background noise was blessedly gone. "Just stupid Jerry. That man comes up with a new game every night. Somehow they all involve layers of clothes coming off."

I grimaced. I did not want to discuss my grandma and her elderly friends playing strip poker or any other kind of card game. "Do you have a second?"

"Sure, honey. What's going on?"

My hand stilled on Daisy's head. "How did you know you were in love with Grandpa?"

"Oh," Grandma said softly. "Well, let's see. He was my best friend, first of all. Yet he made my heart thump wildly just looking at me from across the room. It was like I couldn't take a full breath when he was near me, but when he held me in his arms, I relaxed completely. In a world of overdue bills and domestic terrorism and the atrocity of fucking raisins in carrot cake, he was my safe space."

I meant to laugh, but what came out was more like a strangled yelp. "I love Zeke!" I wailed.

Grandma chuckled. "Oh, honey, I hope so! You married the man, after all."

Daisy whined, worried about my emotions teetering out of control, so I continued petting her head and tried to keep my shit together. "But you know that was more for the inheritance. I mean, I think he loved me when we said I do, and I think I must have unconsciously loved him too, but..."

"Oh, free bird," Grandma sighed. "Even birds who spread their wings and fly most of the day have a nest to come home to. Why are you so afraid to make a home for yourself?"

I used my shoulder to catch a tear slipping off my cheek. "I don't really know what a home looks like. Dad mostly had a bachelor pad that I was allowed to inhabit if I was super quiet."

"Your dad's a fucking idiot, and since he's my son, I can say that," Grandma snapped. "I still grieve over his death, but I was so damn happy to pick you up and take you home with me."

"You were?"

Grandma gasped. "If you have to ask that, then I didn't do a very good job letting you know. I love you, Rainette Shaw. Other than living with your grandpa, the years you lived with me were the best years of my life."

My eyes burned and my nose was actively running. "That's only because Jerry keeps stripping," I teased.

Grandma barked out a laugh, but it ended on a soft sigh. "If you love Zeke, make a home with him. Here or across the globe. Let yourself create the home you two kids want. Fill it with love and you'll be the most successful, and happy, woman I know."

I sat up straighter. Hope inflated my lungs. Maybe the distance I'd been feeling between us wasn't a problem brewing but simply Zeke giving me space to come to a decision. My head started nodding before the ideas had fully formed.

"You're right, Grandma. And I'm staying in Blueball. I just took a job working for Lawson, in fact. I'm going to make a home with Zeke right here. Just you wait!"

"That's my girl! Now go tell Zeke."

We got off the phone and I stood up, looking down at Daisy on the couch. "No time for napping, girl. We have a husband to propose to!"

CHAPTER TWENTY-FIVE

Zeke

I WOKE up the next morning with a solid cramp in my neck. Unlike what I'd led Rainey to believe, I was not hungover. I was dead sober from sleeping in my truck after spending the day at the lawyer's office, Walter & Walter, Esquire. Every minute of my time there had felt like someone was crushing my heart with a trash compactor. When the pain had become unbearable, I'd left the office and driven my truck to the park where I had a partial view of our spot under the bridge. That view did absolutely nothing to help the pain, but I made myself feel it. A punishment of sorts for letting Rainey back in. I ate a mountain of junk food, but I didn't touch a drop of alcohol. The plan was to set Rainey free today, but I didn't want to numb away the ache in my chest. As long as that was still there, I still had a tiny piece of Rainey with me.

Hitting the ignition button once, I checked the time on the dash. It wasn't quite eight o'clock yet, but I couldn't put this off any longer. Plus it would start getting hot in this truck as soon as the morning sun rose fully overhead. I turned on the engine and headed back to the lawyer's office.

Joseph and John Walter were twins. Lookalike assholes. Joseph was the worst of the two, so I tried to mostly communicate with John. They'd quizzed me down yesterday to get all the details in drawing up the divorce papers, but I had a feeling some of their questions were just to slate their morbid curiosity. There was no doubt in my mind that I'd be the center of town gossip by tomorrow, once Rainey had been served with the papers. Client-attorney privilege was the only thing keeping their mouths shut so far.

When John pulled up in his Mercedes Benz and entered the office, I slid out of the truck and stretched my back. Hoping no one would see me go in, I walked through the back door to the office same as I had yesterday.

"Morning," I said to the back of John's head as he fumbled with his old-fashioned briefcase. He nearly jumped out of his Italian loafers and slapped a gnarled hand to his chest.

"Jesus."

"Nope, just Zeke."

John didn't crack a smile and neither did I.

"You know, we have a front door."

I tipped my head. "And you know Blueball."

John sighed and waved me into his office, flipping on the lights and stowing his briefcase under the ornate wooden desk. He gestured to the same leather chair I'd spent a good portion of yesterday in. "Have a seat."

I did, sinking down into the cushions and wondering how I'd gotten here. Why did I have to love a woman who couldn't love me back? Why was I destined to give my heart to her, only to have her keep tossing it back? Why couldn't I have fallen for a woman who wanted to stay in Blueball?

Why wasn't I enough to make Rainey stay?

That right there was the worst question to ask. All it did was send my brain spiraling down into a dark place.

"Did you hear me?" John's harsh scrape of a voice interrupted my self-loathing.

"Sorry. Say that again?"

He sighed like I was too much work for him, and quite frankly, I didn't need his bullshit on top of everything else. "The courthouse filed the papers right before closing last night, so you're good to go on having Ms. Shaw served. You sure you don't want to use our delivery service?"

Their service consisted of a surly teen throwing the packet at someone's head the second they answered the door. Rainey deserved better, even in this.

"I got it." I stood, hand out.

John sighed again, but pulled the packet of papers out of his briefcase and gave it to me. Joseph stuck his balding head inside the office.

"Off to end another delusional marriage?" His fuckin' dentures were too white to even whiff at being natural.

"Off to chase another ambulance?" I tossed back.

That got his damn mouth to shut real quick. He grumbled, heading back to his own office across the hallway. "Women ain't worth it. Not sure why that's so hard for the youth of America to understand."

I shook my head and left the office, heading out the back door again. Joseph Walter hated women, an outlook on life I couldn't understand, even with my heart breaking right now. I'd have to stick Marlo on grump watch, giving her permission to smack me upside the head if I started morphing into Joseph or John Walter in my aging bachelor days.

Sitting in my truck, I eyed the packet of papers on the passenger seat. It physically pained me to look at them. To know that I was ending the one good thing in my life since my father died. I simply loved Rainey too much to tether her to me when she wanted to be free. This heartbreak felt awful, but it also felt a bit like finally sanitizing a festering wound. It was a necessary pain that would allow me to live afterward.

The drive home was a silent one. I felt like each mile marker that clicked by was a countdown to the end of my marriage. Pulling up my driveway and seeing Rainey come barreling out the front door with a broad smile on her face made that final piece of my heart shatter and fall away. She was wearing a pink sundress, the one that made me lose my mind when the short hem danced along her tan, trim thighs. Turning away before I could talk myself out of this, I grabbed the paperwork and got out of the truck.

Rainey plowed into my chest, wrapping her arms around my neck as Daisy ran around our feet, barking. "Good morning! I'm so glad you're home!"

She leaned up on tiptoes to kiss me, and I turned at the last second, giving her my cheek. She pulled back a fraction of an inch to stare at me. All that happiness she'd exuded when I pulled up dissolved in an instant. She released me like I'd burned her, stepping back and eyeing me with suspicion.

"What is going on, Zeke?" she asked on a whisper.

I steeled myself, feeling like the worst human on the planet, yet fully believing I was doing what was right for Rainey in the long term. I needed to word this carefully so she understood I wasn't rejecting her.

"You know I love you, Rain," I started. Her eyes instantly teared up. She looked fuckin' scared and that cut deep. "I would go to the ends of the earth to give you what you want. I married you on a moment's notice to get you that inheritance. And I've enjoyed our time together so much."

"But. Right? There's always a but," she snapped bitterly.

I shook my head. "You've never wanted to live in Blueball. You like to be on the move. You like new places and people. You'd go crazy staying in this same house with me and Daisy."

"No, I wouldn't!" she cried. She stepped forward again, gripping my shirt in her fists.

I put my hand on hers, gently releasing her fingers. "Yes, you would. You used to have an entire spiralbound notebook with all the places you wanted to see. You're still that girl, Rainey. And no one who loves you should tie you down. You should go see all those places. You have the money to do it. Now I'm giving you the freedom to do it."

I reached back into the truck and handed her the packet of papers.

"What is this?" she asked, voice trembling as she held it.

I stared deep into her eyes, knowing the tearstained look she was giving me right now would be burned into my memory forever, haunting me. "I'm giving you your freedom. Sign the paperwork and in six months the marriage will be officially over."

The moment it sunk in, Rainey sucked in a sharp inhale of air. A tear spilled down her cheek and Daisy shifted onto Rainey's feet, whining up at us both. Even my dog could sense this was a tense moment.

"You're divorcing me?" Her voice sounded so small. Like somehow even her personality had shrunk the second I handed her that packet.

"We always knew it was temporary, right? You have your inheritance. Now I'm giving you the freedom you wanted too."

Rainey's teeth bit down on the side of her bottom lip. More tears spilled and her eyes were turning red. But she didn't look away from me. She just studied my face for a long moment and then nodded.

"Okay."

Her face crumpled but she turned and ran, racing up the porch stairs and into the house. Daisy kept whining, torn between running after Rainey and staying with me. I leaned back against the truck and buried my face in my hands. This was fuckin' awful. Daisy leaned into my leg.

Everything in me in that moment searched for a way to take it all back. To go back to living with uncertainties because at least I had Rainey for a short, however temporary, period of time. But as she flew back out of the house with her suitcase and her duffle bag thrown over her shoulder, tears still streaming down her face, I knew this was the only way.

I had to set her free.

The only way I could trust that her love for me was real was to have her choose it of her own free will. Binding her to me with a marriage she needed to inherit her father's money wasn't the kind of love I wanted. Or deserved.

Rainey dragged the suitcase across the driveway and turned away from me. The stubborn woman was seriously going to drag her suitcase all the way into town on foot.

"Rainey. Wait. Let me drive you at least."

"No!" she shouted, not bothering to turn around. "I called Grandma."

"Rainey!" I called after her. We should talk about this. Say goodbye like two adults.

She pulled the strap of the duffle bag further up her shoulder and lifted her free hand in the air, middle finger extended.

Well, fuck.

That was familiar.

CHAPTER TWENTY-SIX

I FELT SMALLER than the little black ants marching along the side of the road, so insignificant that people in their cars just drove right over them, taking out hundreds if not thousands without a single thought. I only made it around the first bend in the road before my knees gave out and my lungs refused to inflate. Embarrassing sobs broke the peace of the morning and I was afraid they were coming from me. A squirrel, frozen on his hind legs when I started sobbing, took one look at me and scampered back into the forest. My suitcase slid out of my hand and wobbled half on the blacktop and half off before crashing to the dirt on its side. I threw the packet of divorce papers on the suitcase, not wanting them in my hands any longer. I sank onto the suitcase and contemplated the ants marching around this new obstacle in their path.

Fingering the empty space on my finger that used to contain two wedding rings—the rings I left on Zeke's kitchenette table just now—I wasn't sure if I was crying because I was sad or because I was angry. It was probably a combination of both. This didn't feel at all like the day I'd found my father slumped over his desk in his home office. I'd cried then because I was scared of my future, not because I was sad he was gone. This...this sensation of my ribs being crushed, the wind knocked out of me, being entirely unmoored from reality and not caring one bit what happened to me...this felt like nothing I'd experienced before.

My phone rang, startling me and halting my pathetic crying. I twisted until I found it in the crossbody purse that had shifted to my back as I dragged my suitcase down the road. It was Grandma calling. I answered, putting the phone to me ear. I even opened my mouth to say hello but no sound came out.

"Rainette? Honey? It's Grandma Gertie. Zeke said I needed to call you. What's happened?"

I bowed my head, pain slicing through me. I even lifted a hand to feel along my chest, certain I'd find a gaping wound there. Of course Zeke would break my heart and then still care enough to call Grandma. And of course he knew I lied when I said I'd called her. If there was one person who knew me better than myself, it was Zeke.

Which was why his rejection felt worse than death.

My own father had rejected me, defying nature itself by turning his back on his offspring. And now Zeke, the man who'd stood before a judge and married me, just to help me out of a rough situation, had reached his limit with me.

I, Rainey Shaw, was officially unlovable.

"Honey? Answer me. Where are you?" Grandma's sharp voice cut through the fog of humiliation.

"Side of the road. Just past Zeke's." My voice came out worse than a frog with a head cold.

"I've got my keys. I'll be there in ten minutes. Stay on the line with me, honey."

So I did. With monumental effort, I kept the phone pressed to my ear, crying not so silently as I wallowed in shame. I'd never been enough for the men in my life. I always caught on to things a little too late. If I'd read my father's disinterest for what it was, I wouldn't have spent the first eight or so years of my life doing things for him to get him to love me. The number of coloring pages I brought home that had an "I heart Daddy" on them was in the millions. By middle school, I realized that he was incapable of love and I quit trying to win his favor. If I'd recognized Zeke's love for me for what it was back in high school, I wouldn't have left Blueball with Hawk. And I certainly would have found a way to love Zeke back. Now that I did love him back years too late, he was already done with me.

What was the phrase? A day late and a dollar short?

That was me. I finally had all the dollars, but I was still too late.

Grandma's old Chevy pulled up next to me, flashers blinking. She hopped out of the driver's seat and ran over, sinking down in the dirt to clutch my face in her liver-spotted hands. When her eyes instantly filled with tears, I knew that was love I saw on her face. Took me way too long to know what love was, but now I knew it was both a wondrous and devastating thing.

"He's divorcing me," I wailed, tears starting anew.

Grandma shushed me, pulling me into a hug. I clung to her. A new realization hit right before she pulled me to my feet. I was finally free. All that freedom I'd been searching for my whole life was finally here.

And I fucking hated it.

"Come back to Skinner House with me. We'll have a sleepover."

I swiped at my cheeks, trying to pull myself together. When Grandma reached for my suitcase, I leaped in front of her, grabbing it and hauling it to the back of her car. I may be heartbroken, but I couldn't let my aging grandma lug around my suitcase. I'd left her in the lurch once before and I'd never do that again. My duffle bag went into the car next and soon we were zipping down the road back to Grandma's place.

"Won't Vander and Marlo mind me being there? I mean, they're Zeke's friends." I sniffled, my nose already feeling raw from all the tissues I'd been using in the car.

"Fuck them," Grandma said vehemently.

"Grandma!" My mouth dropped open in shock.

"What? I love Vander and Marlo, but nobody messes with my granddaughter."

I wasn't sure how she managed it, but a smile graced my face even as more tears slid down my cheeks.

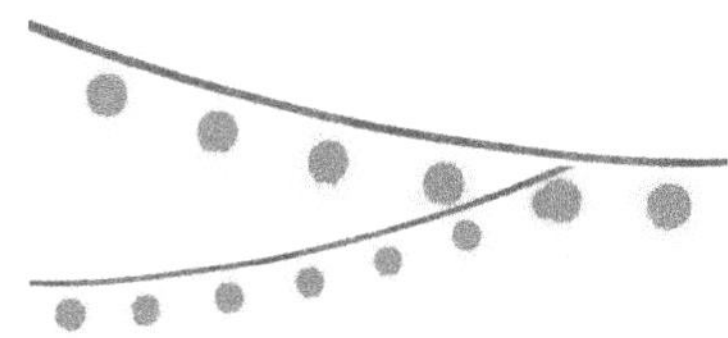

Eight hours.

That was how long it took to wring every last tear out of my body. By dinnertime, I finally stopped leaking out the eyeballs. The pain in my chest was still there, but at least I'd quit crying. My eyelids were swollen and I looked like I'd contracted pink eye, but I wasn't planning on seeing anyone soon, so I couldn't be bothered to worry about it.

The divorce papers mocked me from across Grandma's bedroom, lying innocently on my suitcase. I had yet to slide them out of their envelope and peruse them. Maybe I'd be feeling brave tomorrow.

Grandma had snuck me into the house this morning and even managed to bring me a plate of both lunch and dinner back to her room, though I hadn't been able to eat it. When night fell and she smuggled in three pints of Ben & Jerry's and a sympathetic Milly Booth, we crammed on the love seat under blankets and watched a movie on Grandma's laptop. Despite the reason I was there, sandwiched between the geriatric set of Blueball, I had one of the best evenings I'd had in awhile. Not better than snuggling with Zeke in his bed, but this was a different kind of amazing.

Life on my own as an adult hadn't led to finding friends. I'd mostly worked and slept, trying to make ends meet. I hadn't even realized I was missing female companionship until Milly and Grandma giggled on either side of me when the heroine of the movie slipped in her short dress and flashed the hero.

Maybe it was just *men* who couldn't love me.

I hadn't realized I said that aloud until Grandma paused the movie and swiveled her gray head to glare at me. "You are perfectly lovable, Rainette."

Milly jammed her sharp elbow between my ribs. Did I say I actually liked female companionship? I might have to take that back. "That boy, Zeke, has been in love with you since the first day of freshman year, dummy."

"Ouch," I muttered, meaning both her pointy elbow and her name-calling.

"Did I ever tell you that Zeke was there the day you left Blueball?" Grandma interjected.

My head snapped back to her. "He was?"

Grandma nodded sagely. "He followed you back from the park because he was worried about your safety. After you and Hawk drove away, I went to his truck."

I was horrified, remembering how I'd flipped off Grandma on the back of Hawk's motorcycle, thinking I was the baddest bitch in all of Blueball. More like the dumbest bitch.

"He started crying when I hugged him. I told him to set his sights on someone else. That you weren't ready for him and you'd only break his heart, but he just shook his head. Stubborn man."

Welp, apparently I did have some tears left in my dehydrated body. They were currently blurring my vision and streaking down my cheeks.

Milly tsked lightly. "I don't know. A man who loves like that doesn't strike me as the fickle type. I think those divorce papers are his Hail Mary."

I tried to sniffle hard enough to suck back in the tears and snot that threatened. God, I was a mess. "What do you mean?"

Milly shrugged, that cute little smile on her face that made her the favorite amongst the townsfolk. "In every negotiation, you have to think about what your opponent is thinking."

"Negotiation?" I sat up straighter.

"Oh, honey, marriage is most definitely a negotiation. Maybe the most important one in your life!" Milly chuckled. "So ask yourself. What was Zeke thinking when he presented you with the divorce papers?"

I dropped my head back on the couch cushion and studied the ceiling. "That he was sick of me?"

"Or...?" Milly prompted. "Brainstorm all possibilities right now."

"Or...he wanted to end the marriage that we both agreed would end?"

"What else?"

When I remained silent too long, Grandma piped in with her own idea. "Or he wanted to give you the freedom you've always said you wanted?"

"Ohh, you're getting warmer!" Milly grasped my knee, drawing my gaze to her. "Perhaps he loves you so much he wanted to give you what you said you wanted: freedom. And by divorcing you, he was loving you the best way he knew how."

Grandma nearly knocked the laptop over as she shifted. "And if he let you go and you came back, then he'd know you truly loved him! That's what I said!"

"Huh?"

Grandma grabbed my hands, squeezing surprisingly hard. "That's what I told him when you left Blueball on the back of that motorcycle. I told him that he had to let you fly and pray you came back home. He's letting you fly, free bird!"

"But I don't want to fly!" I shouted, leaping to my feet and dropping all the blankets on the ground. "I want to stay here and build a life with Zeke. Have kids. More dogs. A weekly jam session at Glamper's Paradise. A job. All of it. I'm not running this time, Grandma."

Grandma stood, smiling like she was proud of me. "Good, my sweet girl. Stand your ground and show him the Shaw girls might make mistakes but we also make it right. Stay in Blueball and build that life. With or without him."

I sucked in a deep breath and blew it out. Could I? Could I stay in Blueball and have to see him every day? Could I stay here and have my heart break all over again every time someone said his name?

"Oh God," I muttered. "That's going to hurt."

Grandma put her hands on my shoulders. "You can do hard things, beautiful girl. Besides, he'll forgive you soon enough. That boy doesn't know how to live *not* loving you."

Milly clapped and hooted. "This calls for more Ben & Jerry's!"

CHAPTER TWENTY-SEVEN

Zeke

THE DAYS after I gave the divorce papers to Rainey got blurry. Not because of alcohol, but because I dove headfirst into work, getting to jobsites before the sun came up and staying as long as it took to stumble back home and fall into bed without my brain firing up and reminding me of how much I missed Rainey.

It was the third day, or perhaps the fourth, when I came home, scooped out some food for Daisy, then walked straight to my bedroom to collapse that I realized something looked different. I screeched to a halt in the living room, swiveling my head so hard my neck sent out a sharp pain that pulled me from my exhausted fog.

Rainey's stuff was gone. The items she'd overlooked when she'd left in such a hurry were now gone.

The fuzzy blanket she curled up with in front of the television. The random book or coffee mug she left on the table. The pair of sandals that always ended up where I'd trip over them. I ran to the bedroom, my heart in my throat, then headed to the bathroom. Sure as shit, every single item of hers that I'd planned on keeping forever just so I could torture myself looking at it was missing. I sagged against the doorframe, the sight of my empty vanity and cleaned-out closet like a physical punch to the gut. I'd handed her the divorce papers but I'd held out a small measure of hope that she'd come back. That she'd throw them in my face and yell at me that she was staying. Clearing out her stuff while I was gone at work sent a clear signal of the opposite.

So this was it. She made her choice.

She officially left me again.

The slice of pain was worse this time. Worse because I'd known it was coming and fell in love with her anyway. Worse because I was a grown adult this time and knew the taste of long-term loneliness. I knew what awaited me in the days, months, years of life without Rainey Shaw.

My phone vibrated in my back pocket. I pulled it out, foolishly hoping it would be Rainey. I'd done the same thing every time my phone rang twelve years ago. I'd race to pick up, thinking it might be Rainey wanting a ride back to Blueball. That call never came and this text wasn't from her either.

> Vander: Hey, man. You free tonight? Marlo's got a thing. Thought I'd come over with pizza and beer?

I slid down the wall right there outside the bathroom and tried to think past the whirling thoughts of Rainey. After she left before, I'd retreated into myself. I'd quit being social and buried myself in building my business with my dad. After he died, work had taken over and I liked it that way. The more I worked, the less time I had to think and feel. But I was still damn lonely. No matter how much I wanted to hide and wallow in my depression, I had to choose better this time.

> Me: That sounds great.

Vander: Sweet! Be there in thirty.

I absolutely did not feel like socializing, which probably meant I needed it the most right now. As soon as I felt like I had strength left in my legs, I pushed up to standing and forced myself to take a shower and put on clean clothes. Everywhere I looked I saw Rainey. I wondered if time would erase the memories of her in this house or if I'd have to burn it down and rebuild it just to exorcise her from it.

Vander knocked and came in, not waiting for me to get the door. He was a nosy bastard like that.

"Hope you like anchovies," he called, setting the pizza box down in the kitchen and putting the beer in the fridge, making himself at home.

I walked in and saw him going through my cabinets looking for plates. He pulled two down and turned to shoot me a loopy grin.

"Heard you might need some thick IPAs." He shrugged, reaching back in the fridge to pull one longneck bottle out and hand it to me. "Girls do ice cream, but this'll put hair on your chest."

I frowned but took the beer, twisting off the top and taking a long pull. Every muscle hurt from the manual labor this week, but my heart hurt worse.

"What did you hear?"

Vander cracked open his own beer and got busy plating a few slices of pizza, thankfully without fuckin' anchovies. "Oh, you know small towns. Word travels fast. Gertie mentioned the D word and thank fuck she wasn't talking about dick this time." He cracked up at his own joke, sliding both plates of pizza onto the small kitchenette table and having a seat.

I sat too, wishing I had an appetite. The pizza looked good, but my stomach was still in knots. "I'm sure Gertie got a lungful from Rainey before she left town."

Vander simply grunted, then shoved pizza in his face.

I took another swig of beer. "I, uh, gave the divorce papers to Rainey."

"No shit." Vander didn't put any judgement behind the statement. I wasn't sure if he knew that already or just wanted to hear it from me.

"The marriage was never supposed to be real. I was simply helping her get her inheritance. She had to be married and I couldn't let her marry that asshole who showed up in town with her."

"Of course not. It's far preferable to marry someone who broke your heart over a decade before than to let her marry any other jackass."

I narrowed my eyes at Vander's sarcasm, but he avoided my gaze as he kept shoveling pizza into his face.

"She did say she wanted to date me. And that was after the wedding," I defended myself.

"Definitely grounds for divorce," Vander said sarcastically around a mouth full of pizza.

I was good and pissed now. Just to keep him from eating it all, I also took a huge bite of pizza. We glared at each other, in some sort of weird pizza-eating showdown. We demolished the entire pizza before either of us said another word.

Vander leaned back in his chair and rubbed his belly with a grimace. "Shit, I'm full."

"I could eat another whole one myself," I taunted, unsure why I was attacking my friend but going along with it because it felt good to let off steam.

Vander grinned. "I can't keep up with you working men. I yell at seniors all day and cook them food. Doesn't really work up an appetite like building a fence or something." He hopped up and got us more beers, continuing to chat my ears off about the latest hijinks committed by the seniors in his home.

By the time I started on my third beer I was sure I'd taken the wrong route the last few weeks. I should have been downing beer instead of burying myself in work. The more I drank, the more I started talking, which was weird for both me and Vander. He was used to being the talker and I was used to listening, but the roles soon reversed and we both looked uncomfortable.

Vander finally cut me off by leaving the table to put the plates in the dishwasher and hand me the last beer. "I gotta drive home, so you can have the last one. Plus, you must be parched from talking so much."

"Shut the fuck up," I grumbled.

Vander stood there and smiled at me before slapping me on the shoulder. "Gannon's got you tomorrow. Boston the day after that."

I frowned again. "What are you talking about?"

"We've got a schedule, man. One of us will come each day to have dinner with you, though I have to warn you, those douchebags won't show up with beer better than what we had tonight. I got that shit straight from India."

I turned to look at the bottle in my hand. I hadn't realized the label wasn't in English. "You got more at home?"

Vander grinned. "Fuck yeah, I do. But I have it hidden from the seniors. That and my chocolate. All under lock and key. Be a good boy and I'll bring another six-pack when it's my day again."

As much as I loved the beer, I wasn't down with being the latest charity case amongst my friends. "Call them off. I don't need y'all coming over to check on me like I'm some kind of invalid."

Vander shrugged and squeezed past me to grab his keys off the table. "Too bad. That's what friends do." He spun the keys around his finger. "Maybe after a few visits, we'll have talked some sense into you."

He spun and headed for the front door while I trailed after him. "What do you mean 'talk sense into me'?"

He turned back around at the door. "You're a good guy, Zeke, but you're also a bit of a dumbass. Don't worry. We all were at one time."

Then he shut the door and whistled a tune so loudly I could identify the song from behind a solid wall and door.

"What the fuck just happened?" I muttered to myself, taking my beer to the bedroom and getting undressed for bed.

Sure as shit, every night thereafter, a different friend showed up with dinner and some sort of drink or dessert. They all asked me different questions and gave their own take on the situation. Sometimes I listened and sometimes I didn't. Mostly they just got me talking and I found myself pouring out my feelings like I was a spigot of water that wouldn't shut off now that it had been cranked on. It was fuckin' embarrassing. And yet I didn't want to stop. Not really.

It was strangely nice to open up to friends. Different, that was for sure. I wasn't sure if it was helping, based on the headache that brewed between my eyeballs every morning and the heaviness in my chest that never abated, but it was nice to have company while I was miserable.

The nights were the worst. I would wake up at some point in the early morning hours and not be able to get back to sleep. My body was so tired my limbs ached, but my brain was like a squirrel on crack. I kept going over every interaction, every decision I'd made when it came to Rainey. Ultimately, it all came down to two questions I couldn't answer.

Why was I destined to fall in love with a woman who couldn't love me back?

And how was I going to get over her?

CHAPTER TWENTY-EIGHT

Rainey

LIKE A PHOENIX RISING from the ashes—but with way less grandeur—I poked my head out of Grandma Gertie's room on day three of my sleepover. Grandma informed me the residents would be engaging in a TikTok dance challenge that morning, so I knew the coast would be clear. I headed for the kitchen, needing fiber and water. Grandma was great about feeding me while I'd been squirreled away in her room, but I was starting to have questions about her diet of sugar and more sugar.

I had my head in the fridge, looking for anything that resembled fruit or animal protein when a squeal and a groan broke the silence. I wheeled around to see Vander plopping Marlo up on the island, her legs locked around his waist and his hands...well, his hands were no longer visible, seeing as how they were under Marlo's clothing. I hated to be a buzzkill, but I wasn't sure how to walk out of this room silently before they rounded third base. I cleared my throat.

Vander yelped and Marlo almost slid right off the counter.

Vander ended up steadying her with a hand to her stomach, pinning her to the granite while he aimed an angry expression my way. I held up my hands, one of which had an apple in it.

"Sorry. Hi. I'll just go so you can keep on...doing...things."

"Rainey?" Marlo gasped, pushing away Vander's hand and getting her feet on the floor. Her black blouse was unbuttoned a little lower than she'd normally wear it, but I didn't think I should point that out. As one of Zeke's closest friends, I figured Marlo seeing my face at all wasn't exactly welcome.

"Yep." I shuffled my bare feet, feeling all kinds of awkward. "I, uh, have been staying with Grandma for a few days. Just until I can figure a few things out."

The two of them gaped at me, but Vander recovered first. "You're welcome to stay as long as you need."

"I thought you left," Marlo said right after. "The Wacky Walters spread some rumor about divorce papers and Zeke's gone into hibernating-bear mode, so no one's been able to get him to talk. And since we hadn't seen you either, we figured you left Blueball."

"No," I snapped. Everyone expected me to just tuck my tail and leave. A girl leaves town once and suddenly she's pigeon-holed as a runner? Fuck that. "Zeke served me divorce papers but I haven't left. I'm not leaving."

As soon as I said it, it felt right. It was no longer up for debate. I wasn't leaving Blueball. Not because Zeke dumped me. Not because I was a foolish girl wanting to see if the grass was greener elsewhere. No, I was finally staying because this was my home, dammit, and I had every right to live here.

"Wait, Zeke served you divorce papers?" Marlo's voice had gone so high-pitched Vander winced. "That's it! I'm digging the hole!" Marlo pushed off the countertop, but Vander put his arm around her waist and held her back.

"Hold on there, duchess of darkness. Let's hear Rainey out first, huh?" Vander had to rear back as Marlo reached up with a claw for a hand, acting like she was going to scratch his eyes out. "Save that for tonight, my little black kitty."

My nose wrinkled, but who was I to criticize them as a couple? A girl with divorce papers really had no room to talk. "It's fine. Really. I'm not happy about it, but I don't blame him. I was just getting married to get my inheritance. He was just giving me my freedom like I'd originally asked for."

Marlo untangled herself from Vander, stepping so close she peered down into my face like I was a funny-looking bug she was about to squash with her heavy boots. "But you love him. Don't you?"

I nodded; I couldn't get my throat to release the words. Not to Marlo. If I said them, they'd be to Zeke's face. "Which is why I'm staying in Blueball. I already have a job with Lawson. I figure it'll be torture to stay here and see Zeke, but maybe one day he'll see I'm serious about staying. Serious about us."

Marlo suddenly clapped her hands, that beautiful grin taking over her face. I jumped back. "Go take a shower and get dressed, Rainey. I'll call the girls and bake the brownies. We're going to circle the wagons and come up with a plan."

Vander backed out of the room. "I don't want any part of that. You ladies are kind of scary when you're on a mission." He touched my elbow on his way out of the kitchen. "I'll see if us guys can talk some sense into Zeke. Don't get your hopes up though. His skull is pretty thick."

I smiled, thinking about Zeke, even if that thought also hurt. "I know. It's one of the things I love about him."

"Shoo, woman! We've got big plans to make!"

Feeling suddenly hopeful for the first time in days, I ran back to Grandma's room and showered off the funk I'd been wearing like a cloak the last three days. By the time the girls all showed up, the residents were arguing that Milly only won because she cheated using her cane like a stripper pole, and Vander had to bring out the whistle to get everyone to settle down. We headed out back to sit on the porch with spiked lemonade and a sheet of brownies Marlo had just pulled from the oven.

I had to retell the story of Zeke presenting me with divorce papers and tell them about the inheritance all over again. They seemed to brush over the marriage-of-convenience aspect with surprising grace.

"That boy's in love with you. There's something else going on in that head of his," Paisley drawled, licking her fingers after allowing herself exactly one bite of brownies.

"Seriously," Keva agreed.

"Told you," Marlo smugly said.

Audrey reached over to hold my hand. "You just need to stay and prove to him that this is what you want. Once he knows you mean to stay, he'll rip up those divorce papers. Guaranteed."

I squeezed her hand in appreciation for the support. "Actually, I was going to call you. As kind as Marlo and Vander have been to let me crash with Grandma, I need to rent an apartment. Can you help me?"

Audrey smiled. "Lets go right after this and check some out. We'll get you sorted, girlie."

Marlo tried to force another brownie on Paisley but she wouldn't budge. Said she had to get the baby weight off before they tried for another baby. "Vander said the boys are going to take turns going to Zeke's house and having dinner with him. He might listen to one of them."

"Do you really think he needs that? I mean, once he sees that I'm staying and I have a job, an apartment, he'll change his mind, right?"

Marlo shook her head. "Oh, my sweet innocent dove. That man is as stubborn as those redwoods a few miles up the road. He went down the divorce path and won't change his mind unless we plant some new ideas in that brain of his. I'd bet my favorite excavator that he thinks he's doing something noble."

Paisley nodded. "Yup. Zeke is loyal to a fault. We have to hit this on all fronts. Let the boys do their thing. You get your life set up, and then we'll send him stumbling into your path and we'll see what happens."

I twisted my hands together. I never thought Zeke would push me away, and the fact that he did, had sent me into a bit of a tailspin. "And if that doesn't work?"

Keva shrugged. "Then we regroup. Zeke might be the king of stubborn, but we're the goddamn queens."

Their confident grins boosted my hopes.

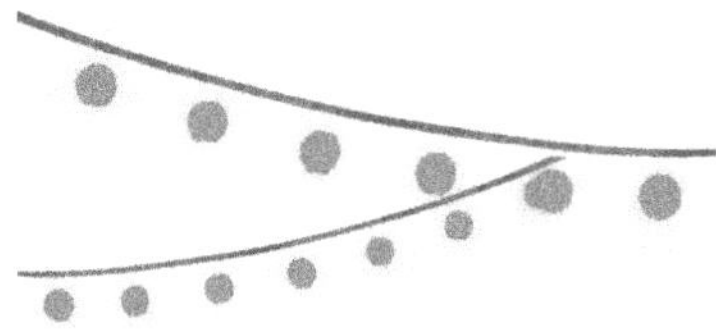

The work wasn't hard, but keeping an upbeat smile on my face was. Lawson turned out to be a good boss, and he'd only trained me on a few tasks so far in the coffee shop, but my thoughts kept a dark cloud hovering over my head. I'd secured a one-bedroom apartment that let me walk to work. Eventually I'd need to buy a car and I had the funds to do so, but I found I enjoyed the walking. People waved hello and I started to say hello back. I was melding into the fabric of this town and I didn't want a sealed car to come between us.

My head was constantly on a swivel, looking for a disheveled brown head of hair and a pair of shoulders that blocked the sunlight. I hadn't run into Zeke yet, but the girls kept me informed of his whereabouts. He'd been working on a job outside of town and then crashed at his house at night. He'd gone into "hermit mode" as Marlo had coined it.

I greeted customers and chatted with Lawson. I nodded hello and traded pleasantries with people in town, but throughout it all, I felt like a shell of a woman. I did everything a friendly person would do, but my heart wasn't in it. There was a part of me that was grieving and always would without Zeke, even as I started to blossom in this tiny town.

It was on my fifth day of my new job that it happened. I had on a pair of skinny jeans, a pink T-shirt with the Crazy Beans logo, and my favorite pair of sandals. My head was down as I walked along the sidewalk early that morning, reading a text from Marlo. The morning breeze off the ocean kept the temperature cool and made this my favorite time of day.

> Marlo: Today's the day.

I started to text her back to ask what she meant, but a shadow fell across my screen and I instantly knew. I felt him before I saw him. My head lifted and all the hope I'd been guarding close to my chest expanded.

Zeke stood frozen in front of me, just a few feet away on the sidewalk. His mouth was slack, his familiar blue eyes wide with shock. There were dark shadows under his eyes, but his hair was a sexy mess like it always was. He looked good in his T-shirt and work jeans, even if a bit tired.

My lips wobbled but managed a smile that I hoped looked unaffected. My hands were shaking, so I shoved my phone in my pocket and curled my hands into fists. Zeke's mouth snapped shut and his jaw flexed, making his cheeks look like they'd been carved from granite by a master sculptor. The man was beautiful.

"Rainey?" His gravelly voice made my heart sing, even as I acknowledged that I'd missed him terribly. "What are you... doing here?"

I swallowed hard and lifted my chin. I'd practiced what I'd say, over and over again until I couldn't possibly forget it. I just hadn't realized I'd be so weak in the knees at seeing him.

"Just because you want a divorce doesn't mean I have to leave Blueball."

His eyes widened imperceptibly. "I thought that's what you wanted. You said—"

The open sign on the door to Crazy Beans clanged against the glass as it was pushed open, cutting him off. Lawson stuck his head out the door. "Is there a problem?"

I shot him a smile. I'd told him everything over a cup of coffee on our break a few days ago, and Lawson had been a good listener. He was not only my boss, but quickly becoming my friend. "I'm okay."

Lawson glared at Zeke, then softened when he looked back at me. "You're going to be late to your shift."

I nodded. "I'll be right there."

I looked back at Zeke, needing just one more minute to soak in the sight of him. Tilting my head to the door, where Lawson had closed it, but continued to stand right on the other side with his arms folded over his thick chest while glaring at Zeke, I moved to go inside.

"I have to get to work, but it was lovely seeing you." That was a lie. It was lovely but it was also torturous. To be so close, but not able to touch him. To not be able to slide my fingers into that thick hair and pull him down so I could kiss him one last time. To whisper how much I loved him and beg him to understand that I was his forever. It. Was. Torture.

The door swung shut behind me. Lawson put his hand on my back and steered me toward the back of the shop, tossing another glare over his shoulder at Zeke through the glass door. Zeke shook his head and then walked away.

"You don't have to do that," I said to my boss.

Lawson turned toward me, an impish smile on his harsh face. "I know, but it's so much fun."

I rolled my eyes and got to work, ignoring the butterflies in my gut that had taken flight upon seeing Zeke. On my break, I texted the girls to let them know what happened. They all agreed it had gone perfectly and we needed to shift into phase two. I had no idea what phase two was yet, but I was sure they'd inform me.

I just knew that seeing Zeke had confirmed everything for me.

I was here to stay in Blueball.

And my heart irrevocably belonged to Zeke.

CHAPTER TWENTY-NINE

eke

I'M A FUCKIN' idiot.

That was the only thing going through my head after seeing Rainey. My hand was somehow on the handle of my truck, my feet taking me there without my brain engaging. I hadn't picked up breakfast like I'd planned when I drove into town before work. I slid inside the truck and slumped against the seat, stunned that Rainey was still here. I'd wholeheartedly believed she'd left again.

She had a fuckin' *job*.

"What the hell is going on?" I muttered to myself. It took me several minutes to understand that a job meant she was truly staying. At least longer than a few days or weeks. When did she get a job? And why was she staying in Blueball? What else had I missed?

Inspiration struck and I cranked over the engine and threw the truck into reverse. The tires left a strip of rubber on Main Street as I headed to Skinner House, disregarding all the speed limits and shocked looks from people I'd known my entire life. Gertie would know. Gertie would tell me all the details I'd missed in my self-imposed isolation in the woods on the work project that was so far ahead I could take a whole week off and still finish in time and under budget.

The truck bounced over the drainage lip in the street as I turned into the driveway of Vander's place. Brain still spinning, I felt like I'd entered an alternate universe the second I saw Rainey standing on the sidewalk. I parked just outside the stone steps to his front door, then hit the steering wheel when I thought about the guys visiting me every night this week. Had they known Rainey was still here? If those fuckers had known but didn't say anything, I was going to have words with them. Who was I kidding? It wouldn't be words, it would be fuckin' fists.

The door flew open and Marlo stood there, a slim column of black in slacks and a blouse that came up to her neck. Even the mug she held to her face before she took a sip couldn't hide the smirk. I bounded out of the truck and up the stairs, towering over her with a glare.

"You knew." It wasn't a question.

Marlo lowered the black mug that said Good Mourning and had the audacity to smile. "Of course I knew. Now get your stupid ass in here."

I growled, but Vander showed up, pulling Marlo behind him. "Hey, settle down, big guy. Gertie's waiting for you in the front parlor. Be nice or I'll have to kick your mopey ass out of here."

I may have been angry and confused, but I'd never hurt a woman or an old person. Maybe I needed to get better control of my face. I tried, but found I couldn't. I was too anxious to know what was happening. How was Rainey still here, and what did that mean for us?

Gertie jumped to her feet when I walked into the parlor. She wasn't smiling or smirking or telling me to get lost. Instead, she just gave me a hug, smelling of joint cream and cotton candy.

"I hear you saw Rainey," she said simply, gesturing to the couch. We both sat and she patted my knee while she perched on the edge of the cushion. "You look surprised."

I gaped. "Well, yes. I assumed she left when she cleared out her things."

Gertie's eyes turned hard. "And why would she have cleared out her things, Zeke?"

Unease creeped into my empty stomach and made me nauseous with the confession that I was sure Gertie already knew about. She just wanted to hear it from me. "I served her divorce papers." Gertie pressed her lips together and I rushed on. "You know how she likes to move around, Gertie. We never intended to stay married. I just gave her what she wanted."

"Why?"

I threw my hands in the air. I'd been asking myself that same question every single day without her. And it always came down to this. "I love her too much to make her unhappy. If she wants to leave, I have to let her go. You said so yourself."

Gertie removed her hand from my knee and sat back on the couch. "That was twelve years ago. Rainey was barely an adult, as were you. Don't you think you've both learned a thing or two since then?"

I was already nodding. "Yes, exactly. I've learned that I can't live with someone who doesn't want me wholeheartedly. I won't settle for less, even for Rainey."

Instead of being angry, Gertie clapped her hands together and grinned. "Excellent. Sadly, your timing was all off. Rainey got that job at Crazy Beans the morning before you gave her the divorce papers."

My view of Gertie narrowed to that of a pinhead. Buzzing rushed into my ear canal and I felt like I was going to pass out. "Shit."

Gertie's laugh was the exact opposite of the crushing guilt that pinned me to the couch. "I'd say so! Rainey talked to me beforehand and told me she had no intention of leaving. She wanted to build a life here. With you. And the start of that was learning to stand on her own two feet, which is why she got the job. And then you shoved divorce papers in her face and broke her heart. That's it in a nutshell."

I flopped back against the couch. "Fuck." My hands were shaking as I lifted them to pull at my hair. I pushed her away, just like her father had done. I promised myself that I'd be her safe space, the one person she could trust, and look what I'd done. "What am I going to do?"

Gertie offered me a plate of pastries from the table. "You go home, think about what you want, and then come up with a plan to win her back. It won't be hard. That girl's in love with you."

I took a croissant and stared at Gertie, hoping she was right. "Even after...?"

She smiled. "Get to know the adult version of Rainey and you'll see she's not fickle. Took her some time to find herself, but she's nothing if not determined."

I jumped up, dropping the croissant back on the plate. "I gotta go find her."

Gertie also stood up, wrapping her bony fingers around my wrist. "Not so fast, buckaroo. You can't go crashing through well-thought-out plans."

Literally nothing about today made sense. "What are you talking about?" That was the problem. I didn't have a plan.

Gertie just smiled like she was about to whoop my ass and I didn't even see the blow coming. "Let the free bird come back to the nest."

I lifted my head to call for Vander. Gertie was either already nipping off the flask she and Milly shared between them when they thought no one was looking or she was having another stroke. Either way, I needed reinforcements. But it wasn't Vander who showed up in the parlor, it was Gannon.

He strode into the parlor with his hat backwards and a Blue-baller baseball tee stretched across his chest. He flashed a smile. "Dude. You're late to practice."

I wrenched my wrist from Gertie's grasp and ran it over my face. Was I hallucinating? Dreaming? Stepping into dementia already in my thirties? What the hell was happening today?

"What practice?" I rasped.

Gannon clapped me on the shoulder. Hard. "We have the softball game tonight against Hell. We need our star pitcher. I know you were all moony over Rainey and you took a few games off, but we need you, man. Get your shit together and let's go practice so we can kick their asses."

"Ohh, the Hellman brothers will be there tonight?" Gertie squealed like a teen girl.

Gannon grimaced. "All five of them. Which is why we need you, Zeke. Come on."

All thoughts of winning Rainey back today were scattered to the wind. I'd have to come up with a plan later tonight after the game, get some sleep, and then tackle this problem tomorrow. I'd have to grovel, make her see that I was only giving her a divorce because I thought that's what she wanted. Surely she'd believe me.

Gannon was a taskmaster, making me warm up and then pitch over and over again until we broke for a late lunch in town. Thankfully, the job I was working on could wait. This fucker kept me under lock and key like he worried I might bolt. We went back to the softball diamond and worked on hitting until the girls showed up with their Blueballer gear and decorations. They strung ribbons from the backstop and tied balloon clusters on each dugout. More of the guys started showing up as the sun began to sink in the sky. I kept an eye out for a short blonde woman, but I never saw her. Maybe Rainey wasn't into softball like she had been back in high school.

"Hey!" Gannon smacked the back of my head. "Get your head in the game."

I turned on him, bumping my chest against his. He was really starting to piss me off. "Who made you captain, asshole?"

He grinned like an idiot. "That's more like it. Take that

aggression into the game. Those Hellman boys piss me off. They think they're so fuckin' pretty."

It was true. They were a handsome bunch with beautiful wives and a bazillion kids running around. And sadly, they were really good at softball. The smell of popcorn and hot dogs from the food cart that got wheeled in every time we had a game made my mouth water. All that practicing had made me hungry.

The game started and I still hadn't found Rainey in the stands. Paisley was on first. Gannon was shortstop, Lincoln was third baseman, and Boston's huge chest made a second backstop as he crouched down as catcher behind the plate. Other guys and girls I'd gone to school with were scattered in the outfield. I didn't recognize the umpire because he was hired from another town to our south to referee this game. Nobody trusted an ump from Hell or Blueball. Not when the two towns had a rivalry going back decades. No one knew what it was over, but every generation kept it going anyway.

We were heading into the ninth inning, tied at four runs each. My uniform tee was dotted with sweat. The sun had long since gone down, leaving us with the bright lights overhead, but it was still muggy out and we were giving it our all. Fuckin' Ace Hellman had hit a home run last inning, gloating as he took his lap around the bases.

Paisley smacked my back with her glove when we took the field. "Look alive out there, Burns."

I frowned at her. I'd been pitching better than I ever had. Probably because I kept hoping that Rainey was here some-where behind the stands, watching me like she had in high school when I pitched on the varsity baseball team. She used to wear my number and taunt the other team, her hair tied back with ribbons in our school's colors. She was half the reason I was a decent pitcher back then. I didn't want to let her down.

Boston walked to the pitcher's mound, a weird smile on his face behind the catcher's mask. "Whatever you do, don't get distracted, okay?"

I gave him the same look I'd given Paisley. "What the fuck, man? Worry about yourself." He cracked up and walked back to home plate without another word.

Why was everyone acting so strange today? And where the fuck was Hell's first batter? I looked over at their dugout, but no one was stepping up to take their practice swings. Then the crowd began to cheer and my gaze shifted to the backstop where the most beautiful woman in Blueball came strutting out onto the infield with a bat resting on her shoulder.

Aha. Rainey Shaw *was* here.

CHAPTER THIRTY

ainey

NOT MUCH IN life scared me. I took the punches when something negative happened and faced everything else with enthusiasm and eagerness. It didn't hit me until I was hiding behind the hot dog stand at the town softball game spying on Zeke and waiting for the exact right moment that the only reason I'd never been scared is because I'd never had something to lose.

And I had a lot to lose right now if this didn't work.

Phase two of the plan my new friends and I had worked out was all on me. While my hands were shaking with nervous energy, I'd come armed to the teeth with everything I might need to sway Zeke to give me another chance. I wore the short denim cutoffs he loved so much. I had his old baseball number painted in blue on my cheek and my lips were as red as a juicy cherry. I'd even had Grandma dig out my old hair ribbons so I could play off those old memories when things had been simpler and our love for each other had been pure and uncomplicated.

Yep. I said it. I loved Zeke Burns. Always had and just hadn't known what that feeling was until it was too late.

The Blueballers took to the field for the "top of the ninth" inning. It was my moment. Zeke stepped onto the mound and I thought I might pass out. My heart beat so wildly I almost couldn't hear Callan Hellman giving me a pep talk. Turned out Hell was all about these grand gestures of love. They ate up my idea when I came to their team practice. They even helped me nail down the details of my plan.

"I was in love with Cricket my entire fucking life, so I get where Zeke is coming from. I promise you, if you go out there and make it clear you love him back, he won't say no. Believe me." He clapped me on the back and then gave me a mighty push.

I barely heard the guy. My feet moved, thank God, and suddenly I was right behind the backstop. I could see Boston jogging back to home plate through the chain-link fence, his smile bright as he flashed me a wink.

"Come on, Rainey. Be a bad bitch and show Zeke what he's giving up."

That was how far I'd gone down the rabbit hole of nerves. I was now giving myself a pep talk. Out loud. In front of the whole Hell dugout.

I straightened my spine, swung the bat up to rest on my shoulder, and just as Zeke began to turn in my direction, I strutted onto the infield like my life depended on it. My hips swayed and my mouth curved into a saucy smile seeing the shock on Zeke's face. The blue eyes I always found such safety in went wide. There was no coldness there like when he'd handed me those dreaded papers, and that gave me courage to keep going. I stopped at home plate, taking up the stance of a batter, and stuck my ass out for all it was worth. If I hadn't been so nervous, I would have preened when Zeke's gaze fluttered to my ass and then back to my face, his Adam's apple bobbing as he swallowed hard.

The crowd quieted down and I opened my mouth to tell him the game had changed. My voice came out on a wobble, but it was loud enough, floating over to the mound where he could hear me.

"If I hit this ball, you owe me a kiss!" Just like that night at the Summer Crawl. The crowd began to murmur and I heard more than a few female sighs.

Zeke's eyes lit the second he recognized the line. He ran a hand over his jaw, and I could have sworn there was a slight tug on the corners of his mouth.

"Why are you playing for Hell?" he called back.

I shrugged, the metal bat cool against my neck. "I figure I need to earn my way back into Blueball after leaving like I did last time."

"You're always welcome here, Rainey." The sweet voice from the outfield came from Rosemary Roberts, the elementary school principal who came into Crazy Beans every morning for her jolt of caffeine before she started her day. I shot her a relieved smile.

Zeke still stood there, looking at me like I was a mirage.

"Are you scared, Zeke?" I taunted.

His lips definitely tugged that time. He wound up and then the ball was flying toward me. I swung—terribly—and missed. The crowd collectively groaned. My lower lip curled into a pout. Boston threw the ball back to Zeke.

"I watched every single one of your pitches in high school," I said loudly enough everyone could hear.

Zeke's cheeks were decidedly pink. He wound up and threw the ball again, an easy lob that even a first grader could have hit. I swung, missing again, but definitely closer this time. The crowd was starting to shout encouragement at me. People I didn't know from both towns were suddenly very interested in me getting a hit.

"Swing faster!"

"Step into it!"

"Strike two!" the ump called, earning him a boo from the crowd. Boston threw the ball back.

"I only get three, right?" I asked Zeke, wrinkling my nose. I hadn't really paid much attention during those high school games. I'd just been watching my best friend. The boy I'd already fallen in love with.

Zeke palmed the ball, studying me. "If it were up to me, you'd get all the chances, not just three."

My heart ached. "I know. That's one of the things I love about you." The crowd hyped up and I had to raise my voice to be heard. I held Zeke's stare, hoping he knew how much I meant every word. And I was definitely talking about more than just this softball game. "But it's time I held myself to a higher standard. You shouldn't have to give me all the chances in the world. I need to get it right this time."

Boston pulled his face guard off and stood. "Here," he grunted, raising my back elbow and showing me how to hold the bat. "Feet apart, and whatever you do, watch the damn ball all the way in, okay?"

I nodded my thanks, trying to hold the awkward position. My hands were so sweaty it was a miracle I was able to hold the bat. Zeke's mouth tipped up into a full-on grin. It was the best thing I'd ever seen.

"Last chance, Shaw," he called out.

I sucked in a deep breath, knowing everything was on the line. "I got this, Burns. Trust me."

The crowd quieted down and Zeke wound up his pitch. Then the ball was flying and everything slowed. The sounds of the crowd faded, the bright lights highlighted the ball spinning toward me, and I knew I had it in me. I swung with every ounce of my power, the bat coming around in a perfectly flat arc. An audible ping and a reverberation that went up both my arms stunned me. I dropped the bat to the dirt and the ball bounced along the field toward Gannon. He made an overly exaggerated effort to get the ball but missed, much to the delight of the crowd.

"Run, Rainey!"

The crowd noise came rushing back in and I wasn't sure what to do. I mean, I knew enough to know to run to first base, but Zeke wasn't at first base. We'd already rounded all the bases anyway, why not take a little detour? So when the entire Hell dugout shouted at me to run, I did.

Right to the pitcher's mound.

Zeke threw his glove down and caught me as I jumped. My legs and arms went around his body and he held me just as tight. I got my hands on his scruffy jaw and knocked the baseball hat right off his head, kissing his cheeks, his chin, his eyes, any skin I could find.

"Please, please, please." I needed his forgiveness, I needed his love. We'd done everything backwards, yet ended up exactly where we needed to be: together. Let him still love me. Please.

The crowd noise drowned out everything except the words spoken in our little bubble. Zeke finally caught my mouth with his, sealing our lips together for a hot, hard, intense kiss that I felt in my toes.

He pulled back just enough to look me in the eyes. "What are you doing, baby girl?"

I beamed, feeling how right all of this was. "What I should have done twelve years ago if I hadn't been such a dumbass. I'm telling you and everyone here that I love you."

The corners of his lips tipped up degree by degree until his face was transformed into a thing of beauty. "Say it again."

"I love you." I threw my head back and shouted it in case he had any doubt. "I love you, Zeke Burns!"

His booming laugh shook my whole body right before he spun us around in a circle. He finally stopped and looked me in the eyes. "I'm so sorry, Rain. I never wanted to divorce you."

I put my finger over his lips. "Shh. I know why you did it. But I choose you, Zeke. I will always choose you."

Something whacked me on the shoulder and we both looked over to see Gannon standing there with the ball in his leather glove. "You're out, lady."

I grinned, tipping my head toward Zeke. "Your pitcher isn't feeling so good. He's gotta go home."

Gannon rolled his eyes. "Get out of here, would you? You're making my wife all swoony and now I'll have to do something nice like rub her feet or buy her flowers to compete with you two."

Zeke carried us off the fields to a commotion I'd never heard during a softball game before. Both teams were cheering us on, and for a brief moment in time, both towns came together for the same thing.

"Congrats, you two!" Callan clapped us both on the back as we walked by, but we were too busy murmuring and kissing each other to notice anyone else.

Zeke didn't let me go until we got to his truck, and even then, he set me down on the passenger seat and kissed me long and hard, his erection nestled between us. He didn't make a move to take things further and it was everything we both needed after being apart all week.

"Take me home, husband," I finally whispered, needing my hands on his bare skin more than I needed to breathe.

"Always, wife." He kissed me one last time and then drove us home, our fingers entwined.

We didn't talk again until Daisy barked her head off and Zeke had to feed her a dozen treats to get her to settle down. Then he stripped my clothes off of me and carried me into our bedroom. I got my wish, my hands skimming over every inch of his skin, my mouth and tongue not far behind. This man loved me unconditionally. Just that thought made my eyes burn with something so pure and good I wasn't sure one person could hold it all. By the time he slid inside me, connecting us physically in a way we'd always been emotionally, there were tears squeezing out of my eyes.

Zeke paused above me, his fingers catching my tears. "You're my first and only love, Rain."

I smiled up at him, happier than I knew a person could be. "And you're my first love too. I didn't even know what love was until you showed me. Now it's my mission to love you just as thoroughly as you've always loved me."

He pulled back and reached over to the nightstand. He came back, grabbed my hand, and slid two familiar rings on my finger. Then he thrust back inside, shivering at the feel of us together at long last. "This is it. You and me, Rain. We're forever."

I slid my hands down to his glorious ass and pulled him into me harder, feeling that metal around my finger and knowing I'd never take it off. Never leave this man's side. Never want for anything beyond his love. "Make me yours, Zeke," I moaned.

And he did.

Three times that night and every night thereafter.

EPILOGUE

eke

SHE COULD HAVE ASKED for a trip around the world and I would have found a way to give it to her. Hell, she could have used her own bank account to make the world come see her, but she didn't. She only asked for one thing and today was the day.

Callan Hellman, a guy who'd come to be a close friend of ours the last three months, was standing in the pergola I'd finally built to be the centerpiece of my backyard. His wife and their friends, Rainey and her friends, had all come together to string flowers over every surface. Shelby, the owner of the florist in Hell, had given us a sweet deal on the flowers, though now that she was nine months pregnant, she had left the actual decorating to her friends.

Half of Blueball and a good portion of Hell jammed into my backyard for our vow renewal service. We kept things simple, requesting everyone bring their own chair and above the sea of faces sitting in all shapes and sizes and colors of chairs was the beaming face of my wife.

Rainey stood in the slider doorway, crouching down and whispering in Daisy's ear. The fluff ball tried to lick her face and then dashed down the stairs, stopping at the center aisle and letting out a bark to get everyone's attention. The Blueball Band of Brothers, the BBB as we called ourselves, picked up their instruments and played an instrumental version of Kane Brown's song "Thank God."

Daisy sauntered down the aisle, her nose in the air like she knew this was an auspicious occasion and she understood the assignment. When she reached me, I crouched down and scratched behind her ears.

"You're my best girl, aren't you, Daisy?" She licked me across the cheek in agreement and then settled so I could get the little box that held our rings unclasped from her collar. We both went back to our places in the pergola and she sat by my side just like we'd practiced.

Rainey came down the aisle in the same sundress we'd gotten married in, the same ridiculously high wedges on her feet, and a bouquet of flowers in her hands. She was tanner this time, having spent a whole summer in Blueball and countless afternoons at the coast. She was exquisite, a mixture of the girl I'd fallen in love with, the woman I adored now, and the soul I'd grow old with. Her ruby-red lips, curved up in a smile, were only for me. This version of Rainey Shaw didn't need attention or crazy plans to have a good time. She still surprised me on the daily, pulling me out of my "old man" habits, but she was grounded in her enthusiasm now. She knew where her heart belonged and she was happy to build a life here with me.

When Rainey finally got to me, she placed the flowers on the ground, and instead of taking my hands, she dipped a hand inside the bodice of her dress. Callan made a choking noise and Rainey shot me a saucy wink. When she pulled out a napkin, wrinkled and frayed at the edges, I knew exactly what she held.

That day at the courthouse I'd given her the makeshift prenup she needed so badly.

She held the napkin aloft. "I don't need this any longer. Everything I have or will have is yours, just like my heart." And then she ripped the napkin in two and let the pieces flutter to the floor.

My eyes got misty and I didn't think it possible, but I loved this woman even more. I'd forgotten about that napkin, but leave it to Rainey to find another way to show me her love. She'd been doing that a lot lately, finding a giddy joy in expressing her love for me, for Gertie, for her friends. It was a beautiful thing to see her blossom.

I took her hands in mine and kissed them. "Thank you," I murmured against her skin.

Daisy inched forward and ate one half of the napkin before I could hiss a command at her to leave it alone. The crowd tittered with laughter. Callan cleared his throat again and began the vow renewal, keeping it short and sweet.

"Do you take Ezekiel Burns to be your husband...again?" Callan asked Rainey.

She gave me another one of her smiles that was only meant for me. "I do, for realsies this time."

Callan turned to me. "And do you take Rainette Shaw to be your wife...again?"

I gripped Rainey's hands tighter. "I meant it the first time and I mean it this time. Every single day that I have breath, I take you as my wife."

Rainey's smile wobbled and her eyes filled with tears.

"Then, by the power vested in me by the town of Auburn Hill, I pronounce you husband and wife...again!"

The crowd cheered, but it all faded away as I looked into Rainey's eyes, seeing my future stringing out in front of me, joy and love instead of loneliness and heartache. I saw kids and laughter and burdens shared. A whisper in the night and a kiss every morning. A thousand chances to show her how much she's loved. A chance to be the man my father had been.

I let her go just long enough to cup her face, to whisper my love for her even though the words weren't even close to being enough, and then I kissed her. We stayed locked together, breathing each other in, until the band started playing a raucous tune and Callan clapped me on the back. The party had started and two towns had come together to celebrate the one thing we could always agree on: love.

We kept the reception informal, wanting to dance and party with our friends and family in comfort. Food was had, drinks were shared, and music was the backdrop to it all. When Rainey complained of her feet hurting from dancing the night away, I knelt to unbuckle those damn sandals she insisted made her legs longer. Then I pulled her to the upright piano my mother had given us as a wedding gift. It had been in our family for multiple generations and some of my earliest memories were lying on the carpet watching my parents pluck out a tune, nestled together on the little wooden bench.

Rainey wasn't musically inclined, but never complained about sitting next to me, learning to play some higher chords that complemented whatever I was playing. Mostly she was there to be my muse. When she was next to me, her scent and warmth seeping under my skin, the words flowed and so did the tunes. I'd already written three songs my friends had been playing at their weekly jam sessions.

But she'd never heard this one.

The guys and I had been practicing it for a few weeks, wanting it perfect for our vow renewal. Vander sang the words, I keyed the melody, Gannon strummed the guitar, Boston plucked the banjo, and Lincoln kept the beat on the drums. The words were about finding love at first sight before you knew what to do with something that big. About fate putting that person in your path again for the reason of healing each other.

We played the last note and Rainey threw herself into my arms, tears on her cheeks. And maybe I was being too fanciful because of all the emotions of the day, but I could have sworn I felt the pat of my father's hand on my back for a job well done.

If you'd like to read a free series epilogue, highlighting where all the men and women in the Blueball Band of Brothers end up...click here (https://BookHip.com/PCJHXZR)*!*

DON'T FORGET *to download Salt Love, a summer romantic comedy romp from west coast to east, featuring a down-on-her-luck woman with a firm grip on her hair straightener now living in the world's worst humidity. Get swept away with the reclusive man next door with secrets galore, a meddling father, and an affinity for kissing his new neighbor. No hair was actually harmed in the making of this RomCom and yes, they really do drive that badly in Florida. This book of self discovery and second chances at love stands alone and ends with a happily every after with just the right sprinkling of flamingos.*

ALSO BY MARIKA RAY

<u>Steamy RomComs - Blueball Band of Brothers:</u>

Grumpy the Bear - Blueball Band of Brothers #1

S'more Than a Feeling - Blueball Band of Brothers #2

Home is Where You Park It - Blueball Band of Brothers #3

Set My Heart Bonfire - Blueball Band of Brothers #4

Pining For You - Blueball Band of Brothers #5

***

<u>All Steamy RomComs Set in Hell:</u>

Grumpy As Hell - Hellman Brothers #1

Bro Code Hell - Hellman Brothers #2

Friend Zone Hell - Hellman Brothers #3

Cougar From Hell - Hellman Brothers #4

Falling First Hell - Hellman Brothers #5

***

Ridin' Solo - Sisters From Hell #1

One Night Bride - Sisters From Hell #2

Smarty Pants - Sisters From Hell #3

Ex Best Thing - Sisters From Hell #4

***

Love Bank - Jobs From Hell #1

Uber Bossy - Jobs From Hell #2

Unfriend Me - Jobs From Hell #3

Side Hustle - Jobs From Hell #4

***

Backroom Boy - Standalone

Steamy Small Town Christmas RomCom:

Grumpy Little Christmas

Steamy Hockey RomCom:

Hot Flashes and Hockey Slashes - Hot Flash Hookups #1

Mood Swings and Hockey Flings - Hot Flash Hookups #2

Steamy RomComs:

The Missing Ingredient - Reality of Love #1

Mom-Com - Reality of Love #2

Desperately Seeking Househusbands - Reality of Love #3

***

Happy New You - Standalone

Steamy RomComs with Delancey Stewart:

The Spare and the Single Mom

Head Over Cleats

Falling For Mr. Safety

Sweet RomComs with Delancey Stewart:

Texting With the Enemy - Digital Dating #1

While You Were Texting - Digital Dating #2

Save the Last Text - Digital Dating #3

How to Lose a Girl in 10 Texts - Digital Dating #4

Sweet Romances:

The Marriage Sham - Standalone

***

The Widower's Girlfriend-Faking It #1

Home Run Fiancé - Faking It #2

Guarding the Princess - Faking It #3

***

Lines We Cross - Nickel Bay Brothers #1

Perfectly Imperfect Us - Nickel Bay Brothers #2

Steamy Beach Romance:

1) Sweet Dreams - Beach Squad #1

2) Love on the Defense - Beach Squad #2

3) Barefoot Chaos - Beach Squad #3

* Novella - Handcuffed Hussy

4) Beach Babe Billionaire- Beach Squad #4

5) Brighter Than the Boss - Beach Squad #5

* Novella - Christmas Eve Do-Over

In case you haven't downloaded them yet, here are my free books!

A JOBS FROM HELL NOVELLA
MAN
GLITTER
MARIKA RAY

ABOUT THE AUTHOR

Marika Ray is a USA Today bestselling author, writing small town RomCom to make your heart explode and bring a smile to your face. All her books come with a money-back guarantee that you'll laugh at least once with every book.

Marika spends her time behind a computer crafting stories, walking along the beach, and making healthy food for her kids and husband whether they like it or not. Prior to writing novels, Marika held various jobs in the finance industry, with private start-up companies, and then in health & fitness. Cats may have nine lives, but Marika believes everyone should have nine careers to keep things spicy.

If you'd like to know more about Marika or the other novels she's currently writing, please find her in her private Reader Group.

If you want to take your stalking to the next level, here are other legal-ish places you can find Marika:

Join her Newsletter -
http://bit.ly/MarikaRayNews

Amazon - https://www.amazon.com/author/marikaray

Goodreads - https://www.goodreads.com/author/show/16856659.Marika_Ray

Bookbub - https://www.bookbub.com/authors/marika-ray

TikTok - https://vm.tiktok.com/ZMJvnQ2Cv